Pauline Johnson
Know Who I Am

a novel

by

John Passfield

Rock's Mills Press
Oakville, Ontario
2021

A Note on Terminology

Such terms as "First Nations," "Aboriginal," and "Indigenous" were not in common usage at the time in which the events of the novel take place. To refer to her mother's people, the historical Pauline Johnson used the terms "English" and "white"; to refer to her father's people, she used the terms "Indian," "Mohawk," and "red." While the novel is fiction, I have used Pauline Johnson's terms throughout the novel in the interest of historical accuracy. —JP

Published by
Rock's Mills Press

Cover Design: Craig Passfield
Cover Illustration: A photograph of Pauline Johnson (1912)
Author's Website: www.johnpassfield.ca
Publisher's Website: www.rocksmillspress.com

Chapter 1

Vancouver by the sea – Vancouver by the sea. My final resting place. A little apartment in a house down by the bay. A room of my own – silver tea-service, a tea-table and some chairs. Things that I haven't known since Chiefswood. Family heirlooms here and there – just enough to remind me that once I had a home.

An old lady watching a young girl.

Chiefswood – glorious Chiefswood. Mother and Father built this home. On the edge of red and white. On the edge of water and land. Ancestral artifacts on the walls. A page in a drawer with our family ties. I stand on the lawn and look up the river and then I look down. I travel on water – I am a canoe. Where will the water and I be travelling years from now?

To be an old chief

A small house on a quiet street.
A palace with a sumptuous ante-room.
A mug full of steaming hot tea.

with the proud name

Is it possible to establish some facts about you?
Certain facts about your ancestral origins?
Do you agree that we start with the facts and then proceed?

of Tekahionwake.

A young boy sitting on a fence-rail.
A man who is beaten almost to death.
A rattlesnake lifting its head to strike.

Meeting Chief Joe Capilano – time has run away with the years. Mutual friends bring us back together again. We renew the bond of London – I have often thought of our meeting when last I was there. A sense of peace in each other's presence – we are both quite fond of tea. We talk of his audience with the great white emperor. Did anything come of their talk? When does anything of importance actually change?

Three Chiefs on a London sidewalk.

A gathering at the family table. Father looks like an English lord. Well – not exactly – not exactly an English lord. Beverly, Eva, Allen – what is each of us going to be? Will we live forever at Chiefswood here on the hill? Or will we each make our way in the world? Move to Toronto – or London? – or Timbuktu? What does it take to go out in the world and make a splash? Mother asks me to stop my dreaming and pass the salt.

A boy was born in Vienna. It was a city of music and romance. Everyone told him he had a talent. Everyone said he was destined to fly. He looked up and saw himself soaring in future days.

"I wonder whether she's American, British, or Canadian."
"I can't tell whether she's Mohawk, English or Mixed."

A story
being told
by a crackling fire.

Keep them at bay - never cease my search - acted as an interpreter - told her i'd be fine - there is no end - is this the way - to learn to make due - look forward to nothing - your very best self - naked dead i.

Well, hello there. Welcome to my home. Come in and sit down.

You are exactly on time. I admire that in a person. I put the kettle on when I saw you coming up the walk.

Oh no, I have nowhere else to go. I assure you I have plenty of time. And I will be glad to tell you whatever you care to know.

What is
the water
in your desert?

Daily walks in Stanley Park. A cup of tea and a cookie with friends who drop by to talk. Canoeing in what I call 'The Lost Lagoon'. Listening to the Siwash ladies as they tell tales of the sock-eye run.

A Norwegian visiting her cousins in Switzerland.

The Grand flows by the house below the bluff. I paddle for hours and days. Thinking of home, thinking of family, thinking of almost everything. What are my roots? – what are my preferences? – who am I and what can I be? If I could go anywhere in the world, where would I go? An observation occurs to me –

paddling down is much more easy than paddling back.

There was a girl who was born in Paris. This girl was born to act. She could play the grandest dame. She could play the ingenue. Every eye in every theatre was glued to the stage.

Moving to Vancouver.
Finding a place, at last, to rest my weary bones.

A story
being told
by the water's edge.

The shadows grew - buffeted and cajoled - whatever pain I feel - in case i get an idea - your approach to life - just passed through - songbird of the red men - in need of my aid - scratch the pen - the questions you sent.

So this is where I live. I call this place my home, although it's what the English would call 'rented digs'. It's the first home I've had since I left what I might call 'my ancestral home'.

'My ancestral home'? Oh that's just a phrase I use. It was a large house that was perched above the Grand River, in Ontario.

But I shouldn't say 'was'. The house is still there. It's just that there are no Johnsons living there now.

A thunder-bolt
from
heaven.

I am a lily – a lily transplanted from pot to pot. I am a daisy – my seed has been carried, by the birds, from field to field. A chance – at last – to put down the semblance of a system of roots. A chance to return some gathered nutrients to the soil.

A beached canoe above a rapids.

Oh I love to sit and read poetry. I bring home arm-loads of library books. Tennyson – Shelley – Keats. *Idylls of the King – Ode to the West Wind – Ode on a Grecian Urn.* The world is all around me – how to put it into words? Not England – oh definitely not England. Words of me – words of my family – words of these fields and flowers and trees. Words of my people – whoever they are – whoever they be.

A young poet arriving in London-town.
A group of miners listening to a recital.
A young girl paddling a canoe.

*Naked born I
into the world.
Naked dead I
from the world.*

You were the thread by which I tried to sew my dreams together. Let me see – let me see. There was dream one – dream two – dream three – oh a dozen dreams or more. I was the needle and you were the thread. And then a snag – a slight tug – and the thin thread was broken. Then a soft breeze came and blew the dreams away.

Do you think of yourself as being a Mohawk?
Do you think of yourself as being white?
Do you think of yourself as having no race at all?

Well, it's time to get ready for my performance. My costumes are here and ready to don. An ante-room in a palace – a broom-closet in a church – a bedroom in milady's mansion – a pin-clothed curtain at the end of a bar. I have every item ready. A little thread-bare, of course, but brushed and washed and ironed. A native princess of the forest – a lady of a Mayfair drawing room. This is what they have come to see. This is the Pauline-Johnson performance. Did anyone notice me as I walked around town today?

*Sun up
open day
I me
child play.*

A girl was born at Chiefswood.

Breathes bravery and life - a taunt more gauling - remembers naught of thee - didn't know billy - teeming with ripe fulfilment - the thought of you - drew the weapon softly - impossible romances - passed it blindly by - you were king of egypt.

*A refusal to ever talk terms of peace.
A target of a thousand rifle balls.
A river rolling along in its rocky bed.*

A well-educated gentleman - conscious of only two things - absolutely level open prairie - do you presume to think - i was made just to sing - crushed and broken - had never been revealed - that I have yet unearthed - i would be the richer - only waters unspoiled by human hands.

There is mention of ancient legends. A casual mention over tea. Oh there are legends? – I am very, very intrigued. I have visited Vancouver – I have performed here many times – but I have never heard any legends that speak of this water and this land. People tell me that the keeper of the legends is my friend, Chief Joe.

A man in a pool of his own blood.

The family dressed in black. Standing in the greeting line. Father so dead – how to believe? Father dead and Mother – alive – leaning on my arm. Murmured sentiments – warming hugs. Too stunned to do more than mumble a simple reply. Life goes on and then it doesn't. Life comes screeching to a halt. Oh what are Father's family going to do now?

There was a girl who was born in Vigevano. This girl was born to act. She was completely absorbed in every role she played. She transformed herself into each and every character. Every eye in every theatre was glued to the stage.

"I wonder whether she's much of a thinking person."
"Well, she thinks, but I wonder just how profoundly she thinks."

A story
being told
as the soup-pot simmers.

Take life quite seriously - take in every word - the depths of our beings - a page in a drawer - we both agreed - what he thought himself to be - the gulf was bridged - nothing came of the plans - a timeless book - his death-song sings.

You seem like quite a self-possessed young man. Have you been a reporter long? You must have decided quite early what you wanted to be.

Sorry to start by asking you questions. I seem to be interviewing you. I have no idea what you want to know about me.

But first, let me make a cup of tea. Then we can settle ourselves down and have a good talk. There's nothing more stimulating to conversation than a nice cup of tea.

Chop the pine
until
you've felled
a mighty oak.

I didn't particularly want to retire – no, I didn't particularly want to retire.

Forty-nine percent of me was happy in my work – fifty-one percent of me said you'd be crazy not to let go after all these years. But there was something that tipped the balance – a thumb or two was pressing heavily down on the scale.

Family mementoes in a cardboard box.

Moving day at Chiefswood. All of our furniture out on the lawn. Goodbye to the family home. A pleasant little house in Brantford. Just the three of us – Mother and Eva and I. Bev and Allen are off on their own. Helping Mother into the carriage. She can't bear to look behind. No, she never wants to see Chiefswood – ever again.

There was a girl who was born in St. Petersburg. Nothing is known about her birth. Was she a peasant? – was she an aristocrat? There are many, many legends. But nothing is known.

Meeting old friends and making new ones.
Quiet talks with my old acquaintance, Chief Joe.

A story
being told
as the kettle boils.

Donned my complete disguise - the current and my paddle - to serve in two roles - what does it take - an adequate form - she kept her secret - the person in the poem - hoping to gain - a broken choice - to clasp thee close.

Yes, I saw the questions you sent. No, I didn't read them at all. I just glanced at them and then I set them aside.

Were you worried that I would say 'no'? Is that why you prepared the questions in advance? Or were you afraid that something important would be left out?

I assure you that I've been interviewed many and many a time. I know enough to protect my interests, if that's what you're worried about. But I also assure you that I have nothing I wish to hide.

Born to fly
but
broken wing.

The Chief is not a man for chatter – he would rather let others talk. Will he share these legends with me? – a person of a different culture? – a person from a different place? If this land is alive with stories, I would like to know.

A person reciting a poem from a stage.

The unveiling of the statue. In honour of Joseph Brant. *Young Canada with mighty force.* A special day in the city of Brantford. *White clouds float hur-*

riedly and high. Sitting on the platform – dignitaries in a row – many words are spoken in honour of this great man. A newspaper reporter busily writing everything down. *Meet we as one common brotherhood.* Mr. Cockshutt addresses the audience. And now, I have the honour to read a very fine poem by our young Indian poetess – Miss Pauline Johnson. *The land is blessed with every good.* I insisted that I was far too shy to read.

"Every life is just as deep as every other."
"The depths of agony, the heights of joy, are in every soul."

An old lady

A girl who is born inside a cage.
A young man interviewing an older woman.
A lady deciding which costume to put on.

who is watching

Do people see you through – at it were – a racial lens?
Do you think that this is a distortion of what they see?
Would you rather they wore no racial lenses at all?

a little girl.

Yes, it is certainly cancer – cancer as sure as sure as sure. As sure as an arrow through the heart. A deer bounding through the forest – drops of blood on leaves and grass. Run as fast as the wind will take you – there is no denying the truth. Every drop of precious blood is dripping away.

A list of extremely urgent questions.

A quiet day in Brantford. To the market and then back home. A letter in the mailbox. Invited to Toronto – to the Young Men's Liberal Club – to read a poem. What shall I read? – what shall I read? What, among my poems, should I read? However, there is one thing that I know – I don't want anyone to read it for me. This time I am determined that I shall read.

Chapter 2

Chief Joe and I – Chief Joe and I walking along. He is puffing on his pipe as he talks. He tells me tales of the Capilano. I have very few Mohawk legends that I can trade. I barely listened when my grandfather talked of the past.

A story being told beside a fire.

Toronto – beckoning Toronto. The town where the poets all ply their trade. Roberts – Carman – Lampman – Scott. Even a female poet or two. And the publishers – oh the publishers. I shall knock on every door. Toronto – challenging Toronto. Doors swing open – doors swing shut. I stand before your doors as simply – Pauline.

To be a young man

A handle which doesn't open a door.
A girl and a boy without a unicorn.
Printing presses whirling night and day.

who brings home

Are you able to read poetry at the deepest level?
Do you feel you have plumbed the depths of the very best poems?
That you have learned poetic technique as a craft?

a new bride.

Drilling assiduously in wood and water lore.
Fingers red with heart blood.
Thieving crows raiding the cornfields.

The old Chief and I are walking along a trail. We stop and look at two peaks in the distance. The Chief has never heard what these peaks are called by other people. The other people of the area have never heard what the Chief's people call these two peaks among themselves. He takes a puff on his pipe, looks off into the distance, and speaks.

A person telling a story to herself.

The Young Men's Liberal Club. An Evening with Canadian Authors. I am far down on the bill, but I am here. *A Cry from an Indian Wife.* Yes I am nervous, but I am determined to read my poem. *Here is your knife.* I peek out past the curtain. All of the faces are bathed in white – and they are male. Leading politicians, leading churchmen – leading editors looking for writers. *Curse to the war.* I clear my throat – I step out on the stage – my voice is full and firm. *His life's best blood.* I look right though my audience to where I am standing at the back of the room – my future me, waiting to hear from my new Pauline. *Starved, crushed, plundered.* I read to the emerging Pauline – to the person that someday I shall be.

He worked hard at his chosen profession. As hard as a horse who is pulling a plough. He studied the works of the greatest masters. The dark of drama – the lofty sublime. If hard work could make him a master, that's what he would be.

"It's like she's putting sunglasses on an ancient Greek statue."
"Or showing an Indian meeting Columbus while riding on a horse."

I tell these legends to her. We sit and sip our tea. She tells me of her grandfather. She always gives me tea in his mug. She tells me she didn't bother to listen when her grandfather spoke. I tell her the legends are never silent, whether we listen to them or not. What story will I tell her today? The rain is running down the window. I will tell her of the time when the waters rose.

Pulled out all the stops - all across this country - the lady in the picture - thinking of almost everything - a failure to appraise - a storm is coming - down to the bedrock - people will see themselves - calling from the dead - how thread-bare.

My ancestry? – oh, you mean my family. I can see where your readers might have a certain curiosity. Though there can't be much about me that isn't known.

Of my family I am very, very proud. My father was a chief of the Mohawks. The Mohawks see themselves as the elite of the Indian tribes.

My great-grandfather was Takehionwake. My grandfather was Sekayengwaraton. Both were also known by the name 'Johnson' – which is, of course, a European name.

What are
the hot coals
under your feet?

Where will the dollars come from next week? Where will the pennies come from today? Perhaps a tin cup on a street corner. Wash some dishes in a hotel. Perhaps I will rent a hall and do some skits and some poems. Perhaps I'll have overflowing crowds and standing ovations. How many miles, in the dust and the heat, to the very next town? I sit and dream – as I often do – of a nice hot bath, a week-old newspaper and a decent meal.

A person judging another person.

Sitting in my hotel room. 'She is the voice of the nations that once possessed this land.' Reading my reviews. 'She is a poet who deserves the loudest applause.' A pair of scissors – a brand new book – a pot of paste. Snipping out all the reviews – yes, the bad as well as the good. 'She would do well to modulate the force-fullness that was so passionately on display.' I am facing the best and the worst – I want to improve as much as I can. 'We greet this young lady on the verge of a promising future.' A hurried note to Mother, in Brantford. She had advised me not to come. No Mother, I am not 'an actress'. I am a 'presenter of cultured verse'. All indications are that I will have – a career.

There was no limit to her talent. She threw her net over every kind of part. Shakespeare – Corneille – Racine. Dumas – Hugo – Rostand – Sardou. She made every role her own.

Enjoying my stationary life, here, in Vancouver.
I make a pot of tea in the morning and sit and write.

I am sleeping the sleep of my dreams. Pelts of wolf – on the teepee floor. A bed in a teepee – on the prairie — a snug retreat from the western winds. I stretch and yawn and turn over. I sleep and so I dream. Am I awake or am I not? Am I in danger or am I not? Am I as safe here as if I was in my own house?

A well-told story - things that I haven't known - i have no stage - a dozen dreams or more - never been a me - look out through my eyes - things are coming to an end - the backbone down the middle - a story being told - right out into the open.

My father was George Henry Martin Johnson. Onwanonsyshon was his Indian name. He was appointed – by his own mother – as a Mohawk Chief.

My mother was Emily Susanna Howells. She was born in Bristol, in England. She came to this continent when she was a little girl.

They were as in love as any two people could possibly be. Thirty years married. Only death could sever them apart.

Sparks and smoke
as it hit
the ground.

In the days before there were mountains, a great man had two fine daughters. They were children who had grown to womanhood. The great man decided to hold a feast – a feast in honour of his two daughters. He invited the people of every friendly tribe.

A traveller moving along a road.

Out on the road as a genuine entertainer. Becoming a writer whose work is in demand. *A Strong Race Opinion.* Being published in newspapers and magazines. *A Red Girl's Reasoning.* Meeting actresses and show-people. Asking for help with my on-stage technique. 'Authors who write up Indian stuff.' Accepting all kinds of offers to come and read my poems. 'Their conception of a people they are ignorant of.' Reading flattering reviews about 'Pauline Johnson – Poetess.' 'The wrongs suffered by her people – the heroism displayed by her race.' Doing everything I can do to promote my cause.

A person who dreams an interesting dream.
A man waking up in a pool of blood.
Two performers leaving town on a train.

Clothing put I
on my back.
Dressing up
and dressing down.

I used to look forward to the talks that we would have. Two sensitive creatures, pouring our hearts out, one to the other, soul to soul. But now – I thank whatever angels nudged our stars out of alignment, saving me from tumbling endlessly through night.

Do you have anyone who can criticize your work?
Who can tell you when it is just not up to snuff?
Who can coach you to a higher level of achievement?

Putting on my buckskin dress. It slides right over my head. No, it isn't a Mohawk dress. I ordered it one day, as anyone else could do, from the Hudson's Bay Company store, in Winnipeg. I sent them a money-order, along with my Brantford address. Looking in the mirror at the mid-calf fringe and the red lining. I have worn it for every performance over the years. Just between you and me, I've had to let it out at the seams a couple of times.

Rise day
make plan
water take
where can.

The girl felt that she was born to write.

Flung their warriors into graves - his flesh is scorched - he will come again - go on the concert stage - mothers every grain - fill my dreams with spendour - while i dream - we did not understand - my tired eyes had need of thee - arrive from lands unknown.

I am the daughter of the great Chief. My sister and I have asked our father for a favour. The war canoes are approaching. There is uneasiness in our camp. Have we betrayed our people to our enemy?

A quill worker embroidering a buckskin mantle.
A death-song on a hot bed of coals.
A lost melody returning from long ago.

An uncivilized savage - buttoned up to conceal - the vengeful lie in her soul - come in handy for an exchange - all that i have written - this united little circle - many thousands of miles from home - one who kept his own life - but the shadow of her story - one must swim in the natural rivers.

There comes a time in people's lives when the ground opens up and people make the decision to jump to the left or to the right. I think that both my brothers did so – Eva, I think, as well. But I – Pauline Johnson – did not. Actually, I jumped back and forth, as the crevice widened out. That was all that I could think of to do.

A pen moving across a page.

Reading – reading – reading. Reading my poems in all the towns. *A Cry from an Indian Wife.* Toronto – Hamilton – Buffalo – St. Thomas – Windsor – Chatham – Owen Sound. *In the Shadows.* Reading everywhere I can. Stratford – Kingston – Fergus – Ottawa – Van Leek Hill. *Ojistoh.* Opera houses – town halls – fancy parlours – school houses – meeting halls. And once, the town Fire Hall. *As Red Men Die.* Anywhere the townspeople come for their weekly culture. *The Avenger.* Asking for sponsors and writing to newspapers – being interviewed in each town – sending posters ahead for boys to tack onto fences. *The Song My Paddle Sings.* New York – New Jersey – Massachusetts. All around the Eastern States. Doing very well at the box-office. *The Pilot of the Plains.* Sending money to Mother and Eva. How are things in Brantford these days? Should I remind them that their advice was to stay at home?

There was no limit to her talent. She could transform herself into every great female role. Shakespeare – Corneille – Racine. Dumas – Hugo – Rostand – Sardou. She made every role her own.

"Well, she's not a conduit for the pristine culture of her ancestors."
"I only hope that she's authentic to herself."

I know he's out there. I know he's trying to get to me. I know he's somewhere in the forest – lost and alone. There's enough moonlight that I can see.
I'm going to go and find him. I can't stay here. He said that he'd come back. I
know he's trying to reach me. He'll know that I am trying to get to him.

As from a chrysalis - nowhere else to go - sealed in the rings - mumble a
simple reply - weighs the balance - the only problem is - not without control - i
thought of you often - here is your knife - mischievous prying eyes.

My siblings all had many names. Henry Beverly Johnson – my oldest
brother. 'Bev' is how I always thought of him.
Eliza Helen Charlotte Johnson. We always called her 'Eva', for short. She
is the one who is living here, in Vancouver, with me.
Allen Wawanosh Johnson, my second-eldest brother. And myself – Emily
Pauline. We were as typical, I would say, as any family could be.

Fish the minnow
until
you catch
a mighty whale.

The two girls approached their father. Father, we would ask of you a favour. You have invited all of the people who live in peace. Please invite all of
the people of the hostile tribe. Let all of these people come and partake of our
meat and our drink. Let all peoples agree that there will never be more war.
Two people pouring out their hearts.
I see the problems of building an act. I cannot carry a whole program on
my own. Teaming up with Owen Smily, a trouper who feels at home on the
stage – who has many techniques to add to my own repertoire. It is incon-
gruous for me to let out a war-whoop and then appear on stage as a gussied
Grande Dame. One cannot always expect an audience to want an evening of
cultured verse. The Indian act goes over well – always passionate, emotional,
loud – but the softer poems are lost on some of the crowds. Above all, I need a
partner – a young male to liven up the crowds – to set me up with an introduction – to give me time to change off-stage. To arrange the itinerary – to book
the halls – to carry the bags – to write ahead for accommodations. To help me
fend off unwanted males, after our readings, among the crowds, as we leave
the theatre by the stage door.

She was taken to the ballet. She was a very fragile child. She was enchanted with the pageantry. It was the spectacle she admired. Every ballerina

was a fairy on the stage.

What is the most 'me' of all the things I have written?
What is the 'me' that I still have left to write?

"Well you had to be dedicated – or had to be crazy – to live such a life as that. Couldn't do it for just the money – that's for sure. A lot of these places were no more than a cross-roads. She played every burg along the CPR. One time, she had to change in a closet. Had to be careful that the candle didn't burn her gown. A lot of places there was no hotel. Stayed at all kinds of peoples' homes. Wife of the Reverend, wife of the teacher, wife of the commander of the Mountie brigade. Everybody was willing to put her up for the night. There was prairie fires and snow-slides and bitter cold and searing heat. Church halls and schoolrooms and meeting houses and bars. Some of the audiences were hostile – some of them ate right out of her hand. When I asked her how she could do it, she didn't reply. She was writing a poem as the train was chugging along. Trying to think of the perfect word, I guess she was."

Did i do my best - an observation occurs - remember the girl - what you wanted to be - if I went back for them - dare to turn around - the aches and searing pains - the current is beckoning - what are the hot coals - extremely urgent questions.

My race? – oh – well, I am classed – legally – as an Mohawk Indian, for government purposes. I grew up in Chiefswood, which both is and is not the Reserve. I spoke English and always dressed in English clothes.

My father spoke eight languages – seven Indian languages and English as well. I never learnèd the Mohawk language, as I saw no need. I only learned what interested me – I didn't see myself as Indian or white.

But don't you get tired of talking about race? Surely your readers have no interest in hearing what I would have to say on that topic. I had plenty of ideas on that issue when I was young – now, it hardly matters what I would say.

Born to sing
but
broken voice.

I am becoming somewhat of a skeleton. The ample paunch that I have carried over what I could term as 'my middle years' is fading away. So what do I see when I look in the mirror? Well, I see what has always been there. Pauline the child – Pauline the girl. Pauline the young poet of promise – Pauline of the London drawing room – Pauline of the cross-Canada tours. There is a skeleton in my future. It has always proudly born the name 'Pauline'.

A person trying on costumes in front of a mirror.

An Indian costume – where would I get an Indian costume? I don't have any Indian clothing, let alone an Indian costume. Very rarely does one see Indian clothing on the Reserve. But it would have to be theatrical – what people think an Indian should be. It is a presentation, after all. A few inquiries among those who study Indian lore. The Hudson's Bay Company – of course. All you do is send away. They have a list of Indian artifacts from which to order. Buckskin jacket – fringed at the sleeves – moccasins with coloured beads. I drop a letter in the mailbox – for Winnipeg.

"She doesn't seem to get along very well with her sister."
"It appears she seldom sees her brothers at all."

A wife

A person breaking through a thicket of brambles.
A whole string of places on a map.
A package arriving in the mail.

who feels trapped

Do you subject your own work to a rigorous standard of accomplishment?
Are you able to read your own work with a penetrating critical eye?
Do you write the very best poems of which you are capable?

in a false marriage.

There was a vote among the peaceful people. Those people are war-like – has the Great Chief lost his mind? He has invited the hostile tribe. But such was the Great Chief's leadership that his warriors lay down their weapons and fished for food – they lay down their weapons and collected the wood for the fires. They looked up and saw the war-like boats approaching. The faces in the war-boats showed great tension. Would there be bloodshed in the midst of the peoples' rejoicing? Was it wrong to invite their enemies to their feast?

A boat approaching an unknown shore.

Heading off to London – heading off to London-town. Pacing on deck in the North Atlantic. Letting the words roll off my tongue. *Eddies circle about my bow.* The home of Shelley, Keats and Tennyson – oh I shall beat them at their game. *Seethe, and bound, and boil and splash.* I have something to offer that none of these poets has had. I have packed my Indian costume – I shall buy ball-gowns when I arrive. *Never a fear my craft will feel.* I have letters to important people. Something new for the London season, Milady? – Milord? The Mohawk Princess will certainly give you your tuppence worth.

Chapter 3

Every word I have ever spoken to others. Every word that has ever been spoken to me. Every thought I have ever had in my head. Every act that I have ever performed in my life. Why do all of these memories come rushing back to me?

Would that my heart could comfort you.

England – oh my England. Taking the day-train down from Liverpool to London. Enchanted by the English country-side. My mother's people might have lived here for a thousand years. Eager to dip my hands in the treasure-trove. A venue for my presentations – a publisher for my poems – a promoter for my talent. To visit the Tower and model the jewels as I admire myself in the mirror – blinking my eyes at the blinding flash. To squeeze my heritage for every drop that it is worth.

To be a young girl

A girl with two suitors for her hand.
Two lovers at the edge of a cliff.
A person drilling upward through bedrock.

in love

What did your great-grandfather, Tekahionwake, pass down as a legacy?

Did your great-grandmother, Catherine Rolleston, bequeath something precious to you?

What do the various streams of your bloodline contribute to you?

with her husband.

Service in Latin, benediction in English, congratulations in Indian.
A trapper filling his pipe and telling a story.
The leaden weight of adversity.

It's ridiculous to grieve your own death. But it's true. When my father died, I grieved for myself. When my mother died, I grieved for myself. When my brother died, I grieved for myself as well. I knew, then, that I was dying too. It's ridiculous to grieve your own death – but it's what we do.

But pure my soul, pure as those stars on high.

I have an idea for a story. Why didn't I think of it before? I have known this story since childhood – it's the marrow in my bones. The story of my mother and my father. Exactly as it happened. Exactly as it was. It's a very powerful story. All the joy and all the pain. Word for word, just as my mother told it to me.

Now in Vienna there was a great composing eagle. Great symphonies were the great composer's forté. Great works seemed to flow from the eagle's pen. From this eagle the little bird took inspiration. He thought that he, too, could soar to the greatest heights.

"She's not a princess – not a Mohawk – not Tekahionwake."
"She doesn't know the Mohawk language or the people at all."

I can feel myself being born! I can feel myself starting to breathe! I can feel my eyes un-peal as I look around! I am born inside a cage! A narrow metal cage! All of life is taking place outside my cage!

I can only hope - a chance to return - the secret was very simple - something that tipped the balance - clear in the mind - looked her in the eye - blood lapping at the shore - responded to the pretense - moving along a road - weigh self in scale.

Yes, I plan to stay in Vancouver permanently. It is very pleasing, after many years of travel, to finally put down roots. I have a few health issues, but I can't see dwelling on those.

I am writing the legends of the Capilano people. They were told to me by the late Chief Joe. In my words, but the story-teller in the stories is an elder who would be about his age.

The legends will be published as a book. Actually, I have two books that I am looking forward to having published. The other is a collection of my stories that have appeared in magazines.

What are
the dreams
that lift you skyward?

Aging? – yes, I am aging. You – the mirror – are always so blunt. No flattery in our friendship – you to I. You who follow me around – recording my face in every hotel. Elegant flophouse or flea-bag palace. The cracks and the dirt, though, I refuse to accept as my own.

I am lost upon the plains.

A little studio in London. The best I can afford. My base of operations. Take the omnibus from here. I have letters to deliver. One to every elegant home. From every prominent person in Canada – to their opposites in London. Please take this young girl in and make her feel at home.

She was the queen of the pose and the gesture. She had a golden voice. Every playwright sent her manuscripts. 'I have written this just for you. It is copied from the play you were in last year.'

Deciding that I will write my mother's story.
I am older, now, than she was when she told it to me.

There is a cage on either side of the cage in which I dwell! There is life in the other cages! There are people on either side! These two peoples are aware of each other, but they are never able to meet! They live on either side of my narrow cage!

The more powerful of the two - a refusal to ever talk - talked of a plan - nothing i wish to hide - offers his eyes to me - then i woke up - the terms so very high - a little sun – a little rain - dressing up and dressing down - who would I be.

My sister, Eva, is visiting me. We grew up together, of course, at Chiefs-wood, our childhood home. I don't know how long she plans to stay.

There's a group of ladies that has been very helpful. Oh, they have helped me in a great number of ways. Sometimes a cookie and a cup of tea is all one needs.

It's the people in one's life that make it worth living, don't you think? I can see – when I close my eyes – every person I have known in my fifty years. I can hear every conversation that I have had.

Everyone thought
that this was the way
things ought to be.

I can't say that I have lived my life without bitterness. I can say that I have fought a life-long battle against it, and have won my share of skirmishes. It is a battle that has been fought on a number of fronts. There is never a final battle in such a war.

The words outleapt from her shrunken lips.

Lydia was born in England. She never had a home. Her father remarried and sent her to boarding school. She was taken to a sailing ship and deposited on the dock. Waiting for her was her father and his second wife. All she remembered in later years were the English bells. Life in Ohio was brutal and stark. Her father said prayers and beat his children. Her step-mother accused her of stealing a cakelet when she had not.

Two snakes who hiss at each other.
A person grappling with a demon.
An item of heritage up for sale.

Wonder who
I am today.
Wonder who
I yesterday.

People don't mention my scars. I don't mention them either. The mirror tells me that my illness is etched quite deeply into my face. More Pauline than I used to be? In some ways, yes – in some ways, no. How could the mirror possibly know? I have a different mirror now than I had on the road.

What did your father, George Johnson, give to you as his legacy?
How did your mother, Emily Howells, influence you?
Has any other person taken a part in creating you?

Putting on my 'English Lady of Mayfair' costume. I have everything here, ready to go. When I am finished, you wouldn't recognize me as the everyday person who just walked in that door. Well, I so enjoyed shopping for dresses in London. My stage-act served as my trousseau. Barker's department store, Derry and Tom's and – wait a minute, let me see – oh, and Pontings as well.

Life ahead
what do
make plan
see through.

She wanted to write about the land in which she was born.

Whose arm was iron - muscles burn and shrink - her dark and dreaming eyes - a robin's whistle in springtime - when feasting is done - pure my soul - the morning of your eyes – soothed our souls to rest - denied the wines of life - never a favour you bestow.

Oh I am Lydia, boarding a ship bound for the new world. My father and step-mother are going to meet me at the dock. What will be my life? What will my life be? A whole new world or the old world following me?

A man with heart of iron and arm of steel.
The screeching of Red River carts.
Tinted leaves, blue waters, fair sky.

A stinging letter from Harry. Yes, I shall think of him as 'Harry', as he presumes to call me 'Pauline'. Harry, the master of the canoe. A reminder of the days we spent in the waters of Muskoka. Sending welcome from all the canoeists in the club. He says he caught my act in Toronto. No, he didn't care to come backstage. He recalls the time when he first heard me reading my poems. He feels compelled to presume on our friendship. What is friendship for, he asks. He begs for forgiveness for what he feels compelled to write. It is a letter which pierces me to my heart.

Medicinal roots and herbs - their coming separation - I have no love for you - faintest dash of native blood - back from the river's brink - the episode of the moccasin - they stand immovable - that purest, most restless river - her legend-land had vanished - could not control the havoc.

My grandfather was a lovely old man. But when he talked, I always had other things on my mind. I was a young girl in a hurry. Does my dress look right? Is my hair in place? Do you think this brooch goes well with this blouse? I have always been concerned with how I appear.
There's a spirit on the river.
Leaving my cards at elegant homes. Being looked down on by the pompous lackeys who guard the gates. 'Pauline Johnson – the Canadian Indian Poetess – Available for Recitals in Drawing Rooms.' Will the door-keepers throw the cards away? Will the dowagers find my exoticism enough? Perhaps the word 'Savage' would fall on friendlier ears.

Her family were theatrical people. She was absorbed from birth in the art. Generations of actors had formed her. She would immerse herself in the roles that she played. She became the character everyone saw on the stage.

"She is trying on every human costume to see how each one fits."
"She feels a kinship with every person on earth."

There are costumes in my cage! They are hanging on a coat-rack! I try a costume on! The bars of my cage begin to move! I slip out through the bars and walk among the other peoples! A different costume for each of the worlds outside my cage! Day after day I put on a costume and move outside in the other worlds! The other worlds are cages of greater size!

Other plans instead - what you want to know - the waters are rising - this

land is alive with stories - felt they knew her - do you agree - plans to mount the
ladder - light up the path - water take where can - caused the flowers to grow.

No, I won't be going out on the road anymore. My performing days are
over – I'm having a much-needed rest. How nice to meet a young writer who
is starting out on life.

You have your whole life ahead of you. Though, no doubt, you have had
a few adventures along the way. I never assume that a young person is a blank
slate.

Go ahead and ask me any question you feel you might want to ask. But
I'm afraid you won't find me to be the subject of 'an explosive exposé'. I have
little to reveal and little to hide.

Watch the moon
until
it blazes
like the sun.

Death comes to everyone. But I'm not saying, watch out, as if you were
standing too far off the curb as a team of runaway horses drags a lumber wagon
along. No, I'm just saying – keep an eye on the clock. Forget to wind it, or turn
the hourglass on its side in the drawer – well, it won't make any difference.
Death, when it comes, is always on time. Death is coming and there's nothing
you can do.

Never a fear my craft will feel.

George was a young Indian lad. He was a Mohawk brave in his prime. He
was an interpreter for the missionaries on the Six Nations Reserve. George
spoke English and the Indian languages – eight languages in all. He served on
the Six Nations Council. While still a very young man he became an Indian
Chief. George worked hard and saved his money. One day he bought a large
estate. He picked a spot above the Grand River and staked out a house.

She was enrolled in ballet school. It was hard for the fragile child. But she
worked and worked at her artistry. She learned that fairies sweat and strain.
She would imagine herself as a fairy as the orchestra played.

I will begin the story as my mother leaves England.
The last thing she will hear will be English bells.

"I think she came alive on stage – it was something she needed – she really did. It seemed to be her way of relating to the world. She had a lightness
– a cheerfulness – that picked up the crowd and coaxed it along. It was an act
they all played together – the blood-curdling war-whoop – the haughty Grande
Dame. These were just characters she was playing – the audience knew she

was just 'Pauline'. She knew they didn't want agony – or social comment – or white man's guilt. She had problems that they couldn't fathom – they had problems that she couldn't know. Would it be agony-for-agony – or smile-for-smile? They were in search of the perfect outing – leave the troubles for a few hours at home. An hour or two of entertainment. It was as if they had winked at each other. The ways of the world could not be changed in an afternoon."

Earn her daily bread - would be left out - on the surface - there is no deny-ing - feel they knew her - the one to carry my name - more original to her - all the pain of the eagle - jumped back and forth - no one who answered.

Yes, it's lovely here in Vancouver. It's a wonderful time for me. A pleasant chapter in what has been an interesting life.

Some days I take a walk in Stanley Park. On other days – be it weather or inclination – I stay inside. Sometimes I read my own poems and stories and legends – some of which have been published and some have not.

Some of my thoughts will never see ink and paper at all. But every thought has been a precious moment for me. I count them as one would count drops on a window-pane.

Choose
the high.
Choose
the low.

Is that my blood on your knife? Yes – I thought it looked familiar. Oh I realize that it's only a few drops. Not likely to be fatal. But it's a few less drops of kindness, of generosity, of hope. A few less drops of the me that you said you found so attractive. A few less drops of the me that I have always wanted to be.

I thought my blessings scant.

Making a break-through in diffident London-town. My highly-placed Ottawa connections are coming through. Invited to a dinner-party at Lady Ripon's. Her husband heard me recite in Ottawa. Reciting my 'Mohawk poetry' as the guests sip their after-dinner liqueurs. The guests are intrigued by 'The Indian Princess'– a 'Redskin' in an elegant dining-room. It's like having Buffalo Bill come to dine.

"She seems to choose such low-level partners."
"They smell of the grease-paint and the stage."

A young boy

A young man trying on a tie.

Two people whose names have been changed.
A person who is betrayed by a word.

who chokes a snake

Do you clearly see who was and was not an influence?
Who has contributed and who has not been a factor at all?
Do you consider yourself to be essentially self-made?

to death.

Every culture has a tempter. Every life has tempters as well. So who have the tempters been in my life? Have I triumphed or have I succumbed? Have I been buoyant or have I sunk beneath the waves?

If I had thought of all the stormy days.

Life at home was intolerable for Lydia and her sisters. Their father beat his children mercilessly. In one hand a Bible – in the other hand, a rod. Lydia's older sister had an offer to marry an older man. He was a minister who was going to move to Canada. Should she marry an older man and move away? Would Lydia be willing to go to Canada with her sister? They had heard that the northern country was still quite wild. The husband was going to work among Indians in the bush.

Chapter 4

We make no attempt to trade meanings – we only exchange the ancient lore. What the stories mean to Chief Joe? – what the stories mean to me? – what the stories meant to our ancestors? Wisdom sealed in the rings of ancient trees.

My duty lies in self-denial.

Finding my way around London. Sometimes sunshine and sometimes fog. Paying out far too much of my savings for London cabs. I can walk my way to an interview – with a publisher or a theatre-manager – but I cannot walk to a fancy mansion in a gown. Effusive praise when I read my poems to the elites, but some of them send a carriage for me and some of them don't.

To be a Mohawk

A little boy dreaming of growing up.
A person writing in another voice.
An arrow which is heading for the weeds.

who is married

Do you read reviews of your books?
Do they have any effect on the quality of your work?
What is the difference between 'a critique' and 'a review'?

to an English girl.

A vengeful lie in the soul.
The land from ocean to ocean.
A child half-smiling at an old woman.

The old Chief came to see me. It was a cold and misty day in late winter. The rain began to fall as he stood on the porch. I helped him out of his great-coat as the kettle boiled for tea. I gave him the big old mug that my grandfather always used. The old Chief talked as we sat and listened to the rain.

Captive! Is there a hell to him like this?

I have no name as a performer. Nor as a writer of poems of note. I am completely unknown in Britain. Can't afford to rent a hall. All I have are reference letters in a sack. To the Marquis of Dufferin and Ava, from the Earl of Aberdeen. Do you remember the girl at Chiefswood? The one who wrote the pretty poems? Her father was the chief who served so well. Could you take her to see Charles Tupper? Could you show her around the town? She'd like to do some recitals. Could you scare up a hostess or two? She's the Canadian Keats – or Shelley – or Tennyson. Dresses up like an Indian when she reads.

But after a while, he thought of himself as the lesser-composer. The also-ran – the not-quite-talented-enough. The eagle soared and soared, but he did not. He became convinced that he was the lesser-bird. The pattern of his flight was close to the ground.

"She's not English, and certainly not a Mayfair Grande Dame."

"And those who should know say that she's not a great poet at all."

I am an expert marksman. My arrow can seek a running deer and find his heart. Keep walking, my precious sister. Keeping walking as you are. I place my arrow on my bow. I draw the string and take my aim. I shall down your cruel captor. My seeking arrow will find his heart. We shall return you to our father who grieves for you.

Every thought and every emotion - one thing that i know - have the best blood - that cardboard box - a blended future - none of their thoughts - one little bread-crumb - nothing i want to say - pouring out their hearts - watch your fading wings.

My health? – thank you for asking. Well – let's just say that I don't expect to die anytime too soon. My health has never been an issue – meaning that my health has never been allowed to intrude.

One deals with one's health – whether of toothache or of heartbreak – as well as one can.

I'd say that my health is still quite reasonable. For a body of my age. I certainly hope to live in Vancouver for many a year.

What are
the nightmares
that suck you down?

A group of ladies comes to see me. They want to make a book. They wish to collect all of the legends that I have told of Chief Joe. They have been reading them in *The Daily Province Magazine*. I give them a title which pleases me – *Legends of Capilano*.

They are all young and beautiful and good.

Invitations breed invitations. Drawing room to drawing room. Lady This and Lady That. I am this spring-season's new sensation. I bathe in the warm applause. You must come to our garden party – your Indian war-whoop curls my hair – you are the greatest poet that Canada has produced. For a fortnight, I have the cream of London society at my feet.

She could play males and she could play females. She would play 'young' and she could play 'old'. The secret was very simple. She knew who her audience came to see. Every play served as a vehicle for her charms.

Deciding that I will write the stories of the legends.
Wondering whether to write them as Chief Joe told them to me.

It's cold here. The wind is whipping across the tracks. The snow is deep enough that there won't be any train. The horse is colder and more exhausted than I am. He can't push through any more snow. When I got back East I was gonna start over. Bury my past and start a new life. I pictured myself on the concert stage. Now I picture myself under ten or twelve feet of snow.

Fairy with limbs of steel - pens and ink and paper - on the surface - wish to tell a story - as if she has a right - a form of farewell - keep oneself mentally sharp - the swan is dying - trying on costumes - the various streams.

I have no fear of death, if that's what you mean. Death gets closer at every stage as we move through life. That we are born to live and born to die is the blunt fact of existence.

It's more a question of how one bears up over the years. How one measures up to the standard that one has set. How one deals with the cards at hand, one might say.

I suppose that the way one deals with death is to look it straight in the eye. Let it come when it may; let it wait around the bend. Live the life that one is granted, day by day.

But there was one
among the many
who didn't take it lying down.

There was just the people, the trees, the fishes, the animals and a few birds. The rain began to fall upon the earth. It rained for days and days and days. It rained for weeks and weeks. The low lands, the treed-slopes, the hills – all of this disappeared. The whole world was being flooded. The people gathered on a high mountain and talked of a plan.

August is laughing across the sky.

On the search for thinking-London. The drawing rooms are devoid of ideas. Having my poems typed to make them more presentable. Where is the publisher who will make me into an author? I want a book – I want a book – I want a book. Thinking-London has thicker doors than the gilded palaces.

A play that makes a sensation on the stage.
A person who feels that she is invisible.
A person who is barely able to speak.

Naked am I
in between.
What I am
and what I seem.

Yes, I am capable of great extravagance. But I am also quite able to live a frugal life. I always order a sumptuous meal when I am flush with cash. When I only have a few pennies, I order more modest fare. Occasionally, I order a splendid banquet sent to my room, with a flattering card. Oh I know who has sent it – it is always me who has sent it. But who would I rather receive appreciation from than my own highly-discriminating self?

Who would you say is your harshest critic?
Who would you say gives your work the easiest pass?
Are you eager to read what each of them has to say?

Well, the neck was a little low for me to wear out in public, as Eva was quick to note. So I fringed it with silver brooches hammered out of coins. These brooches came down to me from my grandmother. No, I didn't know her at all. I have no idea what she would say if she saw me now. I had never worn Indian clothing. I saw very little on the Reserve. This costume is made from whatever bits and pieces I was able to find.

Write things
hope sell
express self
very well.

She wanted to write about the people that she knew.

Whose heart was steel - death's awful brink - scanned the rolling prairie - that voice lives anyhow - lips that love much - dissolve the dark - to soul no harm - my blessings scant - wooed you long - the life that used to be.

I am helping to weave the rope. I work beside the other women. We are making the weave as strong as it can be. The waters are rising as we work. My only hope is to put my child inside this boat.

Death fires lighted on the shore.
Touching a soul in shadow-land.
Unheard, unheeded, inarticulate cries.

Eva and I outside Mother's little house in Brantford. Standing on the side-walk and stopping our talk and saying 'hello' as people pass by. There isn't room inside the house for us to talk without Mother hearing every word. Eva wants to berate me for going out on the road. To ask me how I can sink so low as to go on the stage. She holds her tongue as another neighbour passes. I know what she wants to say. I have heard it all before. It's why my visits home have become so brief these days.

The essentials of living - live in her heart - such a bitter mistake - loves vel-vet and silks - kindness for kindness - the greatest interest in their lives - wing away from the home nest - never heard the name - its waters are perpetually whispering - it is a beautiful story.

My father was very proud. The Prince of Wales was an equal, you see. My father was a Chief of the Mohawk Nation. You know, we'd go out on the Grand – when the ice would break up in the spring. We'd paddle to Brantford or to the Reserve and walk around. And he knew everybody there – everybody we met was sure to say hello. I still have the blanket that he wore in his role as the Chief.

Of man no need has he.

An article on me – Tekahionwake – in a London weekly. The flash-powder pops as I pose and preen. There will be photos of me spread across the page. Explaining to a reporter what the term 'Red Man' means to me. He scribbles as I chatter. I have no idea what he will write. I'll have to buy a paper to know what I think.

The secret was very simple. She chose roles which spoke to her heart. She effaced herself completely. She let the characters use her being as a medium. She became every character she played.

"She coaxes kindness out of some – dampens the fires of cruelty in oth-ers."

"She sees herself as bridging the fissures in human-kind."

I have been called a half-breed. I have no nationality. I belong to no tribe.

I am a thing apart. I have the best blood of the old world in my bloodstream. I have the best blood of the new world in my bloodstream. I will take from this school what is good for me. I will leave in this school what is not good for me. I will move forward into the future on my own.

Doesn't make you unique - all that plodding - hollowed it out inside - thought she was playing herself - i see every drop of blood - laid out in rows - precious, nonetheless, to me - like the waters of the grand - who feels trapped - leaden weight of adversity.

I have had some significant deaths in my lifetime. I'm sure that they have deeply affected me. The death of my father, my mother, my eldest brother – the recent death of Chief Joe.

What we don't think about on the surface – or talk about in conversations – no doubt is active at a much deeper level of our minds.

My grandfather died when I was still a girl. At the time, I mourned – of course I grieved his loss – but there was something that I am still trying to understand. Do you believe that there are people – everyday people in our lives – who mean a lot more than it is possible for us to consciously comprehend?

Dip your pen
in the ink –
oh dip your pen
in the ink.

The people decided to build a boat. It was to be the largest boat that had ever been built. It would need the strongest rope that had ever been made. The men felled a large tree and hollowed it out inside. The women plaited the largest, strongest rope that they could make. And all the time the people worked, the waters rose.

We lift a single daring sail.

Presenting *The Red Girl's Reasoning*. Polite applause in a society-artist's drawing room. Someone remarks that it would make an excellent play. Watching Duse in *La Signora Dalle Camelie*. Wondering how I can make the leap to the London stage.

The ballet did not come easy. Her feet and ankles and limbs were wrong. Her fellow students thought she was awkward. They would taunt her mercilessly. She determined that she would never shed a tear.

Chief Joe and I are the same as human is to human.
We are as different as Englishman is to Turk.

"There was an aura of the Grande Dame about her. The cream had risen to the top. It was a special event whenever Pauline Johnson came to town. She became the talk of the day – 'Are you going to see the show?' The local reporter was flattered to be given an interview. She'd been to London – performed for the Queen – had her poetry published in books. And then when she swept out onto the stage – well, you had to be there. Every movement – every gesture – the Grande Dame in her pride and her prime. You knew that you were present at a special event. She made you laugh – she made you cry – she made you proud of who you were. Made you more tolerant – made you more fierce – made you more angry – made you more sad. Thunderous applause as she took her bows – flowers in season – a big bouquet. Then gone on the train the very next morning and life would go on."

She had hardly known - two as one - life is not life - how to present myself - caught between two rocks - the trails worn down - if you could speak - keep us in the dark - passage through the gloom - what are the dreams.

Do you mind if we get away from this subject? All you wanted to do was ask about my health. It was a courtesy on your part, and nothing more.

Coming to see an aging lady. One with a quiet, sedentary life. Fishing around for topics to give her something to say.

Health – to me – is that which one does not think about unless there is something wrong. Don't you agree? So perhaps we could change the subject and move on.

Choose
the many.
Choose
the few.

Love is not loved by everyone – love is hated by some. Hate is not hated by everyone – hate is loved by some. Life is not life to everyone – life is death to some. Death is not death to everyone – death is life to some. So where does all of this leave you and me?

The groups grotesque on which the firelight plays.

Getting a little desperate. Scouting out a music-hall. Loud, raucous, bawdy. A lot of fun, but not for me. I don't see myself performing on that stage – not a venue for serious poetry, that's for sure. Trying a cockney accent on the way home – just because. The cab-man does it better. My duchess accent is a better fit for me.

"She seems to have no close friends at all."
"Unless you count that old fellow, Chief Joe."

A man

An interviewer being questioned by an interviewee.
A bucket being sent down a well.
A compass as an aid in the woods.

who has to steal

Have you trained yourself to be your own best critic?
Are you able to be a rigorous dissector of the reviews?
Are you writer, editor and critic all in one?

to feed his family.

The boat was completed just in time. The plaited-rope was ready to provide an anchor. The men launched the gigantic boat and the women secured it to a rock so the boat would not drift away as the waters rose. Then they loaded up the boat. A new young mother – a strong young man – and all the children of the people of that time. The young mother sat in the bow to watch – the young man sat in the stern to steer. The waters rose – the boat rose – the children all looked down at their mothers and fathers as the water rose on the land. And not a single person tried to enter the boat.

As some lost melody returning stirs.

I have some good news for you, Miss Johnson. I'm sure you will be pleased. We are going to publish your poems – in book form. About half of them are acceptable. Standard contract – standard royalty – standard price. Of course, your Indian name will be front and centre. T-e-k-a-h-i-o-n-w-a-k-e. We'll have the printer be sure to get the spelling right. Buffalo Bill has created an interest in such things.

Chapter 5

I am not old but I feel old. I am tired and I am worn. I do not have the stores of energy that I used to have at my beck and call. Some mornings I look forward to a walk in Stanley Park. Some mornings I find it a chore to get up and get dressed. Some days I sit and write and other days I simply sit by the window in my chair.

His poor tired eyes in vain have sought relief.

Wondering whether to leave England – my mother's England. Well – not exactly with my tail between my legs. Not hiding, like the poor fox, amid the baying of the hounds, but sitting in my den and comparing my losses and my gains. I have written newspaper articles – good to read and to wrap the fish. I am having my poems published – but in London a book only lives on its latest reviews. I have been taken up as a curiosity – not as an equal, but as an entertainer – and such welcome is no longer-lasting than the soup.

To be an English girl

A person who suffers great pain.
A husband who renounces his wife.
A bird spreading its wings.

who is married

You had, by all accounts, a loving family?
Your life at Chiefswood has been described as 'a pastoral ideal'?
You have met hundreds and hundreds of readers over the years?

to a Mohawk.

Ancient dances, festivals, rites and rituals.
A brother chilled under the icy hand of death.
Bones left to bleach upon the plains.

I shot an arrow through my own heart. I did not know what I was doing. I didn't think that it would hurt. I didn't know what I was thinking. The arrow is gone – I pulled it out. I wiped the blood from off the floor. No one who comes and sips my tea would see it now.

Walk o'er the bed of fire that waits thee now.

Writing the story of my mother. Writing it as a short story – a short story which I will send to a magazine. Now where should I have it start? At Chiefswood, putting roots down, on the banks of the Grand? Earlier roots, perhaps? – Canada, the United States, England? Oh why am I asking such questions? The answer is perfectly clear. I will start where my mother started – write it exactly as she told her story to me.

He could never rise to greatness. Mediocrity seemed his forté. He did not quite have the music. He did not quite have the words. He could never soar as high as the eagle could do.

"She's not a great actress when compared with Bernhardt and Duse."
"She's not a great poet when compared with Dickinson and Keats."

I was born with an interesting secret! I have full control of my eyes! I can look at something and see its inner-depths! I can look at a vase and see how much water is in that vase! I can look at a tree and see whether the rings still grow!

The centre of the world - it was not art - some good news for you - a secret to tell you - standing on shifting sand - a good reader - someone starting out - the heartbreak and the ecstasy - not two stars - the words outleapt.

Marriage? Did I ever consider marriage? Well, let's just say that I was engaged – and then I was not engaged. And that will be enough to say about that.

He was a young man whom I met in Winnipeg – well, of course, I was young at that time too. Career? – racial differences? – change of heart? Which one are you guessing?

Too young to know what we wanted? Later regrets? – or no regrets? – or a little of each? I'll leave you to wonder what the story of my engagement might have been.

Is that scar-tissue
on your back
or the promise of wings?

Prince Arthur comes to see me – the Governor General – the Duke of Connaught. I have the ladies display the red robe that my father wore. Do you remember that day in Brantford? You and I were both so young. Yes, he remembers my father fondly. He gives me permission to use his name in my new book of poems.

Give back the peace and the plenty.

Publication at last. The publisher has made himself a book. The stack of poems I placed on the desk was thrown overboard. The poems paddled their way to the life-boat. Some were rescued – some foundered and drowned. Thirty six poems pulled out of the drink. Not Pauline so much as the Indian half of Pauline. Title – dedication – cover – heavy stress on the Indian themes. Huddled survivors from the ocean-liner Pauline.

She was a diva in her prime. Every play was in service to her talent. She – herself – was every character she played. Every role was employed as her personal showcase. Every author had whittled a flute on which she played.

Sitting and writing the story of my mother.
This afternoon, Chief Joe will come for tea.

I can see everything in its depths! Look at a king and see the skeleton! Look at a chief and see the bones! I see people as they cannot see themselves! People huddle in herds and flocks, but I see us as all the same! I see beneath the flesh and blood to the very bone!

Earned some praise - fissures that scar the earth - tell of who we are - everything went silent - in my on-stage dreams - all the other jewels - experiencing a different day - all standing on a rock - in mirror see - make plan see through.

On the road? Well, you know, I was always welcome in ever home. All kinds of people came to see my act. I played in almost every community in Canada, from coast to coast.

I stayed with the families of farmers, entrepreneurs, cabinet ministers, society ladies and workers in the mines. I made friends – as much as one can make friends on the road – of people of every race and creed. The secret is simply to see each person as an individual person – that's how I saw them and that's how they saw me.

But when you're on the road all the time, you have no roots. You have no community with which to share sorrow and joy. You spend many hours alone in an empty room.

But – surely this is not what you came to hear.

He reared back
and fired some thunderbolts
of his own.

I saw a person on the street the other day, here, in Vancouver. A person I used to know. Did I resist the urge to call out to that person and stop for a while and have a good talk? Well – no – there wasn't any urge. That person would be looking at a person he didn't know. You didn't know me then – you don't know me now. Two ghosts then – two ghosts now. Ghosts walk through each other when they meet. They don't stop and talk.

Wilt thou fail or follow me.

George was a young Mohawk man who acted as an interpreter between the Indians and the missionaries. Lydia was the younger sister. She had come to Canada with her married sister and brother in law. Her role was to help with the children and the chores. There was admiration from the first meeting. She was the best of the English nation. He was the best of the Mohawk tribe.

An audience roaring at a joke.
Boys making comments from a gallery.
A witch who is captured and turned to stone.

Wear I clothing
through the day.
Costume on
and costume off.

Vain and shallow. That is how I think of you these days. Vain about yourself – shallow about me. I had great depths that you were too shallow to explore.

Why did your partnerships come to an end?
Are you close with your siblings now?
Did you not have plans for a marriage that didn't work out?

This is the corset – it's not easy to struggle into, but I have learned to dress with speed. Oh it was a whirlwind when I was shopping – all that time ago – in London. Yes I felt it was worth the money to make things just so. I wanted to act like a Mayfair Lady – not to be one – merely to act. Ever dress-maker had a French accent – real or assumed – and the latest Parisian dresses and fancy hats. Every one of them marvelled that I was so slim at the waist.

Much luck
wish well
day dreams
will tell.

People wondered whether she would write like John Keats.

White star of his life - rest thee here - autumn came and vanished - the last

time I seen him - human-souled - my heart is burning - pierce my feet - all the
storm days - rolls in its rocky bed - shelterless my boat.

I must do this for my son. I cannot be Chief but I am the one to choose the
Chief. I am going to choose my son. He will bring the two together. My son is
respected by both Indian and white.

An old chief telling stories on a rainy day.
A voice that is calling from the dead.
Merry lads and maids husking corn.

Oh Harry – my dear friend Harry. I presume to call you 'Harry', as you
have chosen to call me 'Pauline'. No, I cannot charge you with being 'overly-
harsh'. No, I do not doubt your motives in giving advice. Yes, I feel that much
that you have said has the ring of what you call 'the truth'. Whatever pain I feel
at your words has certainly been due to my 'choice of a life'. Yes, I am the 'two
Paulines' – the two that you saw – a few years apart – on the stage. The one you
'admired' and the one you feel the need to condemn, as of now.

The great life-fight for food - choked a brutal rattlesnake - i did not un-
derstand - imprisoned by some mischance - bullet for bullet - many a sleepless
night - music, pictures and dainty china - the reason it had been applied - his
eyes were dark with dreams - slipped away into the blurred distance.

Bev would be playing the piano. Allen would be sitting and reading a
book. Eva would be sewing a new dress, or darning a sock. Grandfather would
be tamping the tobacco in his pipe. Father would put a new log on the fire.
Mother would stand in the doorway and look around the room.
I wooed you long but my wooing's past.
I feel I have exhausted London – I feel that London has exhausted me. I
have some of what I wanted – some newspaper fame – a short book of poems
– sparkling names in my address book – some contacts on whom I can always
call. Perhaps the biggest gain of all – perhaps the only thing I can claim – is
that I can bill myself on the circuit as 'The Lady-poet Who Was the Toast of
London-town'.

She was a diva in her prime. She put herself in service to every drama.
Every role was the essence of that character. She portrayed their naked com-
pulsions, griefs and joys. While on-stage she – herself – would cease to exist.

"In the US and UK, they scrutinize the works of their minor poets quite
closely."
"In Canada, they sweep them under the rug."

With me there are no secrets! I can see to the depths of our beings! We are skeletons walking and talking! Love is floating like a mist inside the rib-cage! Hate is floating like a mist inside the skull! I am the girl who was born with x-ray eyes!

Tumble like acrobats - huddling over our fate - one in every town - continue his crusade - paying out far too much - just keep writing - thinking of a story - a bullet with your name - the ebb and the flow - until it blazes.

Was I interested in acting? Well, I had a very visible limitation that kept me from the stage. And that was – simply – the colour of my skin.

You can change the colour of your dress – or the colour of your hair – but you can't change the colour of your skin. People just naturally want to see themselves on stage. Perhaps I could have had a long career as a lady's maid.

The day when Desdemona can be black, or Hamlet can be Asian, will be a good day. Sarah Bernhardt has played Hamlet, you know – a female playing a male – but she is a far better actress than am I. I feel that I've experienced all the great roles in my life – Phedre and Medea – la dame aux camelias – but never got to portray them on the stage.

Scratch the pen
until
you've writ
a timeless book.

Once in a while, all the bells start ringing. All the IOU's come flooding in through the door. All the promises – broken and thrown away – knit themselves and jump up and into my lap again. A full house – a generous manager – one of my stories makes a sale. Then there's a pile of ready cash, standing ovations and plush accommodations. One day, I'm up and looking up — one day I'm down and looking up. As far as money goes – it's day by day.

How oft my lonely heart has cried to thee.

There was tension on the Reserve. George was a government interpreter, acting as go-between for Indian and white. He was in line, due to heredity, to take his place on the Council of the Reserve. Some objected that George should not be allowed two roles. But George's mother was 'Chief Matron' and could appoint any male to a vacant seat on Council. She threatened to leave one Mohawk council-seat vacant and there would be one less Mohawk vote on the Council of the Reserve. George was a young man on the rise. He was respected by Indian and white. Despite objections, he was allowed to serve in two roles.

She felt she had great talent. She knew she was willing to work. She absorbed the wisdom of her teachers. She would practice and practice for hours.

When she finally danced in public, she drew much praise.

I sat with my mother, at Chiefswood, as she told me her story.
I can see her face, now, and hear her speak.

"She had a way of cutting across all divides. She'd sat in the room with royalty, you know. And she'd experienced some of the worst of the London slums. People in groups were painful to her. All conflict in the world – to her – was group-on-group. With individuals, she was at home all over the world. All of her friendships – male-female – high-low – red-white – were always a case of one-on-one. She didn't even like to sit in a group of three. The conversation would bounce around, she used to say. Only talk between two people was talk to her. That's why she got along so well with Chief Joe. Neither one of them talked a lot, but they were together for hours and hours. Every single word they spoke would be a gem. The only crowds she loved were the crowds across the footlights, so to speak. The stage was the place where she had some measure of control."

A base of operations - flowing much faster - think of yourself - his the bitterness - i am an expert marksman - i gave them a title - now i picture myself - devoid of ideas - stand before your doors - sit and await my cue.

You seem to be fishing around for a topic – is this the kind of thing you want for your interview? Did your editor tell you specifically what to ask? Oh – yes – I forgot that you sent some questions along ahead.

Well, I only looked them over – what I would call 'superficially'. Some of them could have been quite painful to answer, you know. Not the kind of questions you'd expect a complete stranger to ask.

But go ahead. Ask me any question you want. At my age, what could I possibly have to hide?

But always
born
to face
a broken choice.

I can always tell when people bring me pity. I can see it in their eyes. Every topic of conversation is a blind. They avoid such things as 'how are you' and any reference to my health. One lady brought her little grandson. The little fellow chattered away. Nothing sick about me to him. So absorbed in the penny I gave him. Wondered who was the lady in the picture. Thought it was me instead of the Queen. I'll be dead before he comes again to play.

Calm peace is frighted with my mood tonight.

Seven years went by. George was sure he was falling in love. He did his job and loved the girl from afar. Lydia grew to admire George. He was handsome, intelligent, kind. He was the person she grew to love. They saw each other every day. They never spoke of their growing love. Each wondered what the other one would say.

"She worships her grandfather's memory."
"She hardly listened to his stories when he was alive."

A young man

A cold and windy day on a beach.
Hundreds of poets who are ignored.
Canadians coming together in London-town.

who breaks

Are you one who keeps all people at a distance?
One of those who could be described as 'self-contained'?
What do you think about in the hours when you are alone?

his parents' hearts.

What do the tempters want? What do the tempters want from me now? Your best self, Pauline – your very best self. A performing poet – a published author – the toast of the literary world. We are tempting you to become your very best self.
Their aerial career unseen, unknown.
The boat-train to Liverpool. Turning my half-awareness away from the drizzly landscape. I wasn't offered a suite of rooms in Buckingham Palace, but I found the welcome warm at ducal soirées. No offer from any theatre in the West End. Not enough weight to carry a night on the legitimate stage. London thrives on the new and the different – and new and different is only for once. I have a book, I have an act, but I have no stage on which to stand. Where can I be new and different day after day?

Chapter 6

Every tide-pool has its story – every mountain has its tale. People have lived here – on this land – for thousands of years. Sat at the campfires, cooked the meat and told the tales. Tales of the hunt of years ago – tales of the hunt for the meat and the fish that we eat today.

Take her passage through the gloom.

Planning a Canadian tour. At home in Brantford and leaving again. My mother's house seems so tiny after the places where I have been. An interview with the *Brantford Expositor* – 'Brantford Shines on the World Stage'. Sly digs from my sister, Eva – why not stay home and look after Mom? Tragic despair from my disappointed mother – how could a daughter of mine sink so low as to perform on the public stage?

To be a son

A young person arriving in a big city.
Boys tacking posters onto fences.
A girl searching in the night-time forest.

who acts

Do you agree that writing is tied to a particular era?
That one writes the kind of poems that are acceptable now?
That the current stable of writers is tied to time?

despite his parents' pain.

Sweeping tempests, leaping waters and raging storms.
A man who is shot trying to return some lost stores.
A canoe heading towards a far rapids.

Why does the river laugh and sing? I asked the old Chief. Now it chuckles as a young girl newly in love – now it cries as of a young thing caught in a trap. He settled back as I poured the tea – hot and steaming in the mug. He told a tale that he had heard while just a boy.

Dancing a war dance to defy his foes.

What did I hope to get from my visit to London-town? – what was the honey I hoped to extract? I hoped to become a welcome guest at all levels of society – a celebrated performer of my own works – a social commentator of note – an author of a distinguished published book. I hoped for every faculty of which I am possessed to be allowed to blossom forth at its highest possible level – to be the fireworks that burst in the sky over London-town. I hoped to become the ideal version of Pauline. And now – I am no longer in London-town.

What to do? – what to do? There was nothing else to do. He was born – he felt – to write music. But great music was not his forté. There were horses pulling cabs all over town.

"She's not accepted by the Canadian or the British literary coterie."
"They let her know that she would never be invited inside."

My parents disapprove of this marriage – she does not know our culture – the children you share with her could never be appointed Chief – she does not carry the blood of the ancient tribe. Her parents disapprove of this marriage – she would be giving up her culture – she would dwell 'mid an alien people – the children would not know who they are. We have talked for many hours. We have tried to talk ourselves out of being in love. We have decided that we will marry no matter what.

A field of sunlit wheat - amazed at the power - what would she think - could never be replaced - helping to weave the rope - the emerging pauline - she often told herself - uncertain candle-flames - in the silent places - the fragile child.

Ah yes – *The Song My Paddle Sings.* Well of all my writings, that has certainly been my most loved, my most requested, my most enjoyed. I suppose it will be the one to carry my name – people quote it to me everywhere I go.

Yes, I wrote that poem in my canoe. I used to canoe quite often on the Grand. I kept my canoe, all summer, on the flats below the house.

I wanted to capture – a mood – a feeling – a sense of life. I had a writing-box – I still have it – with pen and ink and paper – which, at that time, I took with me in my canoe. I stopped paddling, and sat and scribbled, and let the canoe find its own way down the stream.

Not two stars
who
lit up the heavens.

The ladies come to see me. The book is almost ready to go to print – but there is one little thing we've been meaning to ask you, they say. We don't believe that the title, *Legends of Capilano,* will have a wide-enough appeal. How does *Legends of Vancouver* sound to you?

Those hollow hungry eyes that glared.

Exhilarating chats with Owen Smily – rehearsing in Toronto for our new act. Getting publicity-photographs taken – blinking my eyes at the blinding flash. There are footlights all over Canada! – the railway has opened things up for us all! Your fame in London is a calling-card! – your poetry book will give us class! We can tour Canada! – coast to coast! There's a drought of entertainment! – even the tawdriest act is welcome in the West!

She didn't make her audience feel more deeply. She didn't make them think more highly. None of their thoughts was for more than just the moment. None of their tears would do them any harm. She gave her audiences the gleam of shiny bracelets – she let the boring actresses dig for deeper veins.

I wonder who will see themselves in these stories.
See these stories as the stories of their lives.

Sittin' on a fence-rail. My dad expects me home. Spent the whole day huskin' Indian corn. Got the money in my pocket. Dad says we need it bad. He says that's why I gotta work all day. They had a lot of different workers. As I work, I hear 'em talk. Someday, I'm gonna leave an' go far away.

Stand before my god - a slight exaggeration - a hole in my beached canoe - below the line - effaced herself completely - facing the best and the worst - my most probing interview - guiding with her lamp - dig the bones - making a break-through.

I always liked to do something old. I always liked to do something new. At every performance, the people were waiting for that poem.

Perhaps I was a victim of my own success. When I wrote new poems, I had trouble fitting them in. I had so many poems that people were eager to hear.

The critics complained that my act was – let us say, 'thread-bare'. But the people disagreed. How could I drop that poem and substitute something else?

Put your hand
on my hand
and my blood
will start to flow.

An old man and a young man lived on opposite sides of the canyon. There had always been bad blood between the two. Years of fighting had led to hatred – hatred had led to thoughts of revenge. Now, the old Chief had a young daughter. The young Chief across the canyon had caught the young girl's eye – and the young girl had caught the young Chief's eye as well.

And you hear a voice responding.

London – London – London. Why did I ever go there? I was a tourist like hundreds of others. Westminster Abbey – Hampton Court – the dome of St. Paul's. I waited outside the gates, at Buckingham Palace, for the Queen to come out and wave. Taken up as a curiosity – presented in lavish drawing rooms – but there was no offer from any stage. Published a book, for which I am grateful – even some flattering reviews – but my poems were seen as charming ducklings, not as swans. Each hello was a form of farewell. Why did I ever go over there? I was glad to get back home and start over again.

A young girl peeking through a curtain.
An old man with two fine daughters.
An actress looking at herself in a mirror.

This my face
in mirror see.
Change it to
another one.

There are some people I can see right through. Other people are as opaque to me as a wall. I need a partner with a head which is made of glass. I want to see every moving part in the workings of his brain. No mysteries, no surprises, no games to guess or to fail. I've had my fill of mysterious strangers – the rocks on which my emotions have been torn. For my partner, I want a mechanical wind-up doll.

Do fashions in poetry inevitably change over the years?
Can a writer rise above the current limitations?
Can a writer of our time write lasting works?

The silver brooches do double-duty. They serve to secure the ermine tails. Ermine is highly prized in Europe. Those ladies pay dearly for what Indian ladies no longer wear here. No, no – of course I didn't – no, I didn't trap them myself. If I hadn't inherited them from my grandmother, I would have purchased them from a store. I have never trapped a wild animal in my life.

On stage
please crowd
feel good
feel proud.

People wondered whether she would write like Percy Shelley.

To work him wrong - disdains to touch - the season of the rains - lie awake a-nights - dark in the lost lagoon - calm on all but me - we two dreamed to-gether - how leaden was the weight - runs swifter now - anchorage not meant for me.

I am growing very old. My two sons are one half of me. My daughter is the other half of me. I have lost my only daughter. I stand and look across at the land of my hated enemy.

Fashioning canoes, arrows, paddles and snowshoes.
A girl who seeks her lover in the drifting snow.
The ebb and the flow of nature's pulse.

Eva and I in the house where she works. We are together in her employer's kitchen. Outside the window, there is a garden, laid out in rows. "He'll bring you down, you know. He will." The kettle whistles. My partner is waiting, on the back stoop, for a cup of tea. "And the two of you travelling – everywhere – unchaperoned. You are a poet – Pauline – a poet. You don't belong in a music-hall. Those grubby ruffians only come for his jokes and his smut." Her whisper has the hiss of a jealous snake. "This creature is so vulgar, so crude, so – vaudevillian." The kettle steams as she spoons out the tea-leaves. "He'll bring you down to where you're not a poet at all."

Ancient dances and festivals - winding and lashing itself - to salve his own sick heart - blood for blood - went forth on his crusades - real tortoise-shell combs - quick eye saw the resemblance - his heart was brimming with tales - look in the silent places - the wind will blow free for me.

My mother couldn't look at the house. Chiefswood– where she'd lived for thirty years. All the furniture was out on the lawn. It was an auction sale – she was moving to a tiny house. The porch was where she'd found my fa-ther – drenched in blood. All she took was a few pieces of furniture and some cardboard boxes with things like the tea-service – the one that I have with me now. Eva and I did all the packing – the boys had long ago left home. She wore her funeral dress so everyone could see. She couldn't wait to get in the carriage and drive away.

You'll take that name right back again.

The CPR – the CPR. Drawing all of Canada together. Our life-line across the land. We are welcome in every community. A church hall – a pool hall – a rough-hewn concert-hall in the woods. Every building with an open floor that can serve as a stage. And the people in these settlements – they are starved for entertainment – they are starved for a night of culture. They work so hard and save their pennies – they overwhelm us with applause. They beg us to come back when we board the train. They are the reason that I have chosen the life of the stage.

She sought to make her audience feel more deeply. She raised them to a higher level of thought. None of their thoughts was merely for just the moment. Their tears were for the agonies of the world. She was an actress who aroused their hopes and their fears.

"Her work will get its due in a hundred years."
"Or perhaps a little longer – we will see."

Not one buffalo on these trails. Badger holes – gopher holes. Herds of antelope – a coyote or two. A band of riders with repeating rifles. The prairie grasses blow in the wind. There used to be thousands of buffalo on this prairie. Grazing as far as the eye could see. Just the trails worn down by a thousand hooves. We'll never see the buffalo again.

Simply trust me - would never sell - sit in judgement of me - every tide-pool - you had to be there - two sensitive creatures - graft on these ancient bones - burn into its core - my tired eyes - who chokes a snake.

A professor came to one of my shows. He asked me about the poem. He wondered what *The Song My Paddle Sings* meant to me.

What was the paddle? What the canoe? What was the water? – what the eddies? – what the flow?

Everything stood for something else. The paddle could not be a paddle – the canoe could not be a canoe. The professor wanted to know what each of these 'images' meant to me.

Dig the bones
of a hopeful
future.

The young Chief shot an arrow that landed beside the young girl – the young girl shot an arrow that returned his regard. The two exchanged their tokens – shell beads and ermine tails – each one pledging to be together until the end of time. One day the young Chief met the girl on her father's side of the canyon and led her to his home. The old Chief and her brothers searched for the girl in vain.

That bursts its chrysalis in scorn.

'Not enough weight to carry a night on the legitimate stage.' That's what they told me in London. Oh if they could see me now. We have been all across this country. We have been welcomed in every town. And the poems that were rejected – they always ensure the greatest applause. They didn't have enough faith in their readers. Good readers can make a poem come alive. They put themselves inside the book as I do when I read.

She had advice which never left her. 'Never imitate anyone else. Take an inventory of your weaknesses. Know your strengths as well. Never try to be anyone but who you are.'

The waters and the landscape of Vancouver.
The waters and the lands where these stories will be read.

"She would always laugh – yes, she would – about the engagement. Laugh and say it didn't matter to her at all. She was too busy with her career to bother to marry. No – the mixing of the races didn't matter to her – her mother and dad were proof of that. There was acceptance in both families. The best of both from the friends on both sides. No – there was nothing in Pauline's life that affected her so little as the end of her engagement. It was no set-back and no disappointment. She would always laugh whenever the topic came up. But there was little cause for that– it was hardly ever mentioned. No – to my knowledge she never saw him again – although they were both living there in Vancouver near the end of her life. She always brushed the topic aside with one of her smiles."

Where to place her - the water is so low - how would we manage - not know who they are - be a rigorous dissector - looking in the mirror - nothing as grandiose - only audience is me - held under tension - all the storm days.

We were standing in the hall. A church in one of the prairie towns. We were talking as the people filed out the door.
"Well, I'll tell you, Professor," I said. The professor's ears were on high alert. A number of people stopped leaving and gathered around.
I recited the whole poem again – line for line and word for word. Those were the only words on that topic I cared to say. They told him exactly what the poem meant to me.

Pour oil
upon
the ocean.

Where does cancer come from? What does cancer want? Give a little – give a lot. Give everything you can give – and then some more. And cancer is right back – knocking at your door.
My tired eyes had need of thee.

The Queen – the Queen – the Queen. Every interviewer is eager to ask about the Queen. Which poem did you read? What was Her Majesty's response? What is she like in person? Did she laugh or did she smile? It is my partner's favourite story. It is the gem-stone of his every interview. The day that he and his assistant – Pauline – entertained, at Buckingham Palace, for the Queen. A speck of dust in a ray of sunshine. Sparkling brighter than all the other jewels in his crown.

"She seems to revere her father and her mother."
"It's an ideal that sours her view of everyone else."

A girl

Two performers rehearsing in an empty hall.
Rain running quietly down a window.
A girl pasting reviews into a scrapbook.

who is abused

What, in your work, do you feel will come to be seen as dated?
What in your work, do you feel, will stand the test of the years?
How will your work be regarded a hundred years from now?

by her father.

One day, the vengeful brothers saw their sister in the distance. She was walking with the hated young Chief on the canyon's rim. The silent water of the river flowed beneath – it had never made a sound in all its years. Then an arrow was placed in a bow and held under tension – the arrow-head sought the young Chief's heart. Just then, the young girl stepped in front of her lover – her brothers' arrow sped towards her on the air.

Would that my soul could see.

I can't think of a better way to spend my life. The railway has opened up this country. Performers can travel from coast to coast. I can work and perform in Canada for ever and ever, it seems. I have a partner who knows the business. My poems are well received. People take me into their homes and offer to put me up for free. Just keep writing those wonderful poems. That is all we want from you. It's the beauty of the people – it's the beauty of the land. You are the one who speaks for all of us. Your poems say what everybody feels.

Chapter 7

Soon my life will be at an end. Did I do my best with what was available to me? Will I enter the grave with a smile or with a frown? Pull the turf over my being and snuggle under its warmth? Feel that, all in all, I have had a reasonably-good day? Close the eyes and think only of sleep? Look forward to nothing but peaceful sleep for a thousand years?

Will reawaken all my depths of pain.

Oh, I should be at home in Brantford. A letter from Eva was at the desk, waiting for me. The usual barbs against my profession, but a new note is added this time. Mother is ailing – Mother is ailing – she often wishes that you would come home. Is this a ploy from devious Eva? Is mother actually in need of my aid? We are so busy here on the road. We are booked in every town along the CPR.

To be a wife

A performer with an idea for a performance.
A bird wondering where to make a nest.
A golden locket on a chain around a neck.

whose husband's life

Is it true that you made a number of trips to London?
That you had letters of introduction to people there?
How many trips to London have there been over the years?

is in constant danger.

A train stopping in the middle of a Blackfoot Reserve.
The grief of desolating fire and human pain.
Scant blessings and few mercies.

You must have learned a lot in your travels, he said. He looked a lot like a doctor, or perhaps a lawyer, down on his luck. I suppose I have, I said, though I cannot think of a single example right now. The wisest thing I can think of to say is that I might have learned about the same by standing still.

Still he dances to death's awful brink.

It's been accepted by *Mother's Magazine*. They want to break it into four parts. The others say that it's not quite what they want. Of course they only want a certain kind of story. They tell me they prefer to 'zero in' on their 'pre-ferred clientele'. As I read the letter, I expected that it would be another rejection. I'm sure they bought it for the sentiment – they didn't buy it for the grit. I can only hope they'll print it word-for-word.

Perhaps a partnership, he thought. Perhaps he could write an acceptable libretto. A libretto for an opera which the greater-composer would write. There were talks – there were many discussions – but nothing came of the plans. The mighty eagle continued to soar alone.

"She's had to keep going further West to find an audience."

"She keeps repeating her successes – never deepening her act or her poetry."

I visit my sister once in a while! I let a year or two go by! My sister lives on the ocean floor! In the lea of a sunken ship! The bubbles rise to the surface as we talk! She always tells me she has everything she needs!

Need a bigger stage - deserves to be a sensation - that was for someone else - even the tawdriest act - half of them are acceptable - sending posters ahead - enough to remind me - the scars of forest fires - my soul could see - lie in the soul.

So what – exactly – is your 'angle'? Yes, it's newspaper jargon, as you would know. I told you I've given many interviews.

'An Exotic Indian Princess in a Mood of Reflection in the Glow of Her Sunset Years'? 'An Aging Vaudeville Trooper Takes Stock as the Footlights Fade to Black.'? 'A Flamboyant Grande Dame Spins Fabulous Tales of a Long and Extraordinary Life'?

I never sit down to write unless I have first made a plan. Surely you have some expectations that brought you here. Just what are you hoping to gain from this interview?

Just two sparks
who
winked in the night.

Walter McRaye comes to see me. He is bursting with spectacular plans. As soon as your books are ready, Pauline, I will write letters to everyone! – I will insist that they buy your books! I will give interviews in newspapers! – reminisce about our glory days! If even one person in every town and village and hamlet buys a copy! – as a souvenir of our wonderful shows! – why you'll be able to paper these walls with dollar bills!

You have stolen my father's spirit.

I work my way through the list. *Ojistoh – As Red Men Die – A Cry from an Indian Wife.* My Indian segment is the more powerful of the two. I want them to see what I can see – I want them to feel what I can feel. But it isn't all war-whoops and blood and revenge and pride. There's a lyric note to the evening. All is quiet – a pin could drop. Then I lead them through *The Song My Paddle Sings. The river slips through its silent bed.* Someone told me that poem is almost like a hymn.

Her audience wanted to share her glamorous lifestyle. Feel as if they were visiting in her home. She was the lady that they knew from the Sunday papers – the stage was her personal salon. All were invited to spend an evening with their favourite celebrity. Every patron in the audience was a personal friend.

I hope that people will see themselves in this story.
Two young people who fall in love across a divide.

The pull of the tide is gentle here! Gently it rises – gently it falls! Tiny fish drift by in schools! My sister waves to them with smiles! She tells me she has everything that she could possibly need!

Resentment on both sides - the surface is a cartoon - it's the one regret - the workings of his brain - if thinking causes pain - prairie fires and snow-slides - anything of importance - will sing no more - is this the way - is there a hell.

It's been a long and fruitful life. A long and enjoyable life. A long and productive life.

On some topics, I don't want to go into details. Some topics I discuss, but you notice I keep it brief. And for other topics, I gladly give free rein.

Oh no – I'm not sorry that you came. No – I love a good interview. Would you call what we have here 'a duet'? – or perhaps 'a duel'?

Caress my heart
with your heart
and my heart
will beat as well.

His mother loved me. His sister loved me and I loved them. My mother and my sister overwhelmingly approved. Now – what in the world, I thought, could possibly go wrong?

But forgetting all, she follows.

George's parents arranged a marriage. With an attractive Mohawk girl. This was designed to keep the blood-line pure. George refused the arranged marriage. He had other plans instead. He told his parents that he wanted the freedom to choose on his own. George left his parents' home. He went to see the English girl. He asked the English girl if she would be willing to marry him.

A woman who is drifting in her thoughts.
An old lady smiling at a young girl.
A person prodding another with a sharpened stick.

Speak my lines
upon the stage.
People hear
the chosen me.

'Make-do' has always been my watchword. That is the backbone down the middle of my affairs. At times I have pushed myself forward – at times I have held myself back. At times I have been held down – at times I have been buoyed up. I am a bubble who has floated on many a stream.

Did you expect to be welcomed by the writing community?
Did the publishing community treat you as you felt you deserved?
Did you expect to find a place on the London stage?

Believe it or not, I can tie the corset behind me as easily as you please. Oh the satins and silks of London – I had such a time to choose me a dress. Finally I simply had to decide – they were about to close the store. A dinner-dress of brocade – cream was the fashionable colour that year. And a bustle that seemed to stick out forever behind. A busy, cheerful seamstress made me four dresses to bring back home. These farm-women simply swoon when they see me on stage.

Make friend
much joy
fall love
lose boy.

People wondered whether she would write a major poem.

His pride as highest - fling unto him the choice - listened for his coming -
the great big blizzard day - savage of breed and of bone - outspread, laggard

wings - days marvellously fair - workworn and old - eddies circle round my
bow - cursed my soul.

I am thinking of my son. I do not want to, as it is causing me great pain. I
always did what my parents asked of me. I was loyal to my tribe. And now our
son is causing my wife and I great pain.

A man being beaten with a beech hand-spike.
A man giving another man his horse.
Corn bursting out of its chrysalis.

Eventually, Harry, there will come a day when I can stop the touring and
end the 'shallowness', as you so bluntly call it. Yes, there is going to come a
day. That will be when my poems are appreciated, as I know they will come
to be. I am writing some new poems now. They have the same kind of 'fresh-
ness', I believe, that led to your early praise. What you see on stage is what
a poet has to do – to 'stoop to', as you say – if she is going to earn her daily
bread. The day will come when I will stop touring and turn my hand to more
'serious work'. That will be the day when my poetry starts to sell.

Fighting, hunting, food-getting - the whirr of many wings - a bunch of
dead daffodils - listening to the rain - wandering on the edge of a chasm - their
loves were identical - the haunting memories - some ancient poetic supersti-
tion - the channel that leads to the yesterdays - as though they searched the
future.

Oh Bev – my brother, Bev. I thought of you often but seldom met you. We
seemed to have so little to say. You lived in a city. You had a job. You had no
family. That was all I needed to know. All the rest – your friends and your ac-
quaintances – I did not care to know. My travels swung me near your orbit and
flung me far. I hope that all was sunshine. We never talked of negative things.
We always – always – met on neutral ground.
But self-encrusted I had failed to see.
Now a smile at something I've said. And now a tear at the situation of
one of my poems. *A Cry from an Indian Wife*, for instance. That was a tragic
situation. I was only fourteen when that happened – a truly tragic situation.
My family suffered through it as if we were living there. John A. Macdonald
– Louis Riel. Just where did our loyalties lie? A mother came up to me after
I read that poem – she waited to talk to me – white skin and tears in her eyes.
She said she'd never thought of what it was like for the other side.

She never plastered her face with youthful makeup. She let all her natural
flaws and wrinkles show. All her acting was in her voice and in her expres-
sions. She could break a heart with the tremor of her lip. Every thought and

every emotion was there to see. People felt that they had met her on the street.

"I wonder if her writings have that incandescent glow."
"Her writings and her life, together, will light up the room."

I talk to my sister – she talks to me! Tiny bubbles leave our mouths and float to the surface! She tells me of her life in the lea of the sunken ship! I tell her I have swum around the world! She tells me she often wishes that I would return and stay at home! All the time we talk the current is beckoning me!

Not a booking to be had - a dreaded scourge - an alternative life - his eyes are seeking - lost my only daughter - scrutinize every page - i only learned what interested me - whatever you care to know - a thousand raindrops - a story being told.

Do you know what I have learned? That people are simply people. Famous writers are just people, after all.

May I make a small suggestion? Why not let the fame go by? Write your article with none of the 'Grande Dame' trappings at all.

A younger person interviews an older lady. The older lady tells what she feels she has learned. Perhaps the younger person would care to give his views.

Dig the bones
of a hostile
past.

I see an endless corduroy road. Towering trees on either side. Gnarled oaks – singing furs – jaunty maples – graceful elms. An endless avenue. Wild fruits – game – flowers. Quail – woodcock – snowy-breasted partridge. Horses hooves padding the dust. The squeak of heavily-laden axles. All the birds are the same as the birds we had in New York.

I may not all your meaning understand.

George's parents were shocked and wounded. How could he stoop to marry a white? How could he let the bloodline be sullied by foreign blood? Now his children would not be royal. They would not have pure Mohawk blood. His children and children's children could never be Chief. Thousands of years of Mohawk pride. Thousands of years of blood and of bone. George was shocked that his parents had been so hurt.

She became a principle dancer. Rose through the ranks with seeming aplomb. People raved that she was inhuman. A tiny fairy with limbs of steel. The dancer was so ethereal – she was almost nothing at all.

What did my mother want me to know?

What do I, Pauline, want my readers to know?

"I think she saw how shallow it all was. Accepted as a Mohawk – rejected as a Mohawk. Accepted as a white – rejected as a white. Deep down, she knew she was just 'Pauline'. Pauline – the girl who liked to dress up and recite poetry that would curdle up your blood or bring a smile to your lips or a tear to your eye. I always felt that was why she played so many characters. She responded to the pretense with a pretense of her own – she would play all the characters that she was never allowed to be."

Every human quality - sewing on a patch - the tracks ahead are cleared - our life-line - is paying dividends - all you do is send away - how to put it into words - a man who was blind - a story that will change - what are the nightmares.

Oh – did I recite for the Queen? – is that what you came to ask? Well, that's always been a rumour. Promoters like to use that phrase when they advertise.

Yes I did go to London. Yes, I hoped to read my poems before the Queen. It seemed the best way to climb the ladder of poetic success.

I had letters of introduction – even one from the Prime Minister of Canada, if you please. Now how do you think it all turned out? Do you think I got to read my poems for the Queen?

Pour oil
upon
the fire.

I don't want anyone to weep for me. I never wept for myself – well, not too often anyway. And when I did, I soon felt that I was wrong, and shook myself out of it. You scrape your knee – you break a fingernail – you fall over into your grave. No – it doesn't make you unique – and it doesn't make you tragic. Manna falls, sometimes, unexpectedly, and at other times, it doesn't. A little sun – a little rain – and life is gone. Save your tears – you mourners – for those who are still alive.

And life lacks nothing, so complete it seems.

Sitting on a bench in a meeting hall in the Kootenays. Waiting for my partner to walk over from the hotel. An old fellow is nursing a newly-made fire. Slightly chilly, but I snuggle in my shawl. Miss Pauline Johnson, ladies and gentlemen! Direct from the legitimate stages of London, Paris and Rome! The greatest Cleopatra of our time! If Shakespeare were here, he would be the first to applaud!

"As far as I'm concerned, she's a mystery."
"I don't think anyone really knows the true Pauline."

A boy

A writer scribbling at dawn.
An island on which nobody lives.
A doctor who gives a final word.

who perishes

What were your plans when you made your trips to London?
What did you hope would actually happen at that time?
Did your writing improve or diminish after the London years?

under a layer of snow.

Thinking of Mother as I darn a sock. A big thick woolen sock as a bulwark against the prairie cold. How did Mother become so timid? To leave England – to leave Ohio – to decide to marry her George. Why is she so against my spending my life on the stage? And Eva – devious Eva – how can I trust the notes she sends? Is mother's illness an Eva-ploy to draw me back home? Now where in the world did I put that other sock?

And all is still at last.

Lydia's younger sister was completely against the marriage. This was a sister whom she had hardly known. She had married a minister and moved to Toronto. The sister implored, the sister entreated, the sister sneered, ridiculed, stormed. Marry an Indian? – how could you? Think of your children and the lives that they will lead! The sister's husband refused to discuss the matter. He ordered Lydia out of the house. Not another night will you spend beneath this roof!

Chapter 8

Walking along with Chief Joe. The waves lap gently at the shore. My old friend does not look well. His face is drawn and his eyes are seeking to hide his pain. What is wrong with you, my friend? Not a question that either of us asks. Better that 'life' should be the topic of our days.

I only claim the shadows and the dreaming.

Canada is such a vast country. New settlements are opening up all the time. It's a great country to write about. A boy was sitting on a fence-rail as the train went gliding by, just outside the little village where we had just done our show. I always carry my writing case – pens and ink and paper – so I got it out and thought for a while and the lines just started to flow. I'm calling it *Joe*, though I don't know his name. *A little semi-savage boy of nine.* Reading it over and changing some words. I'll read it on stage tonight in the next little town.

To be a young girl

Two young people who fall in love.
A person scribbling a hurried note.
A waiter delivering an extravagant meal.

who is bound

Are you touchy about your age?
Is it fair to say that you are about fifty years old?
Would most people not say that these are 'the middle years'?

in captivity.

A rope tied to an enormous boulder.
A roaring torrent filled with broken ice.
A man lying under the stars in sinless sleep.

The old Chief sits beside me on the deck of the steamer. The steamer weaves in and out of the islands of the North. He draws on his pipe and looks out to the sea. He points with his pipe to a misty island in the distance. He looks at my eyes and at my skin. There is a legend, he says, of the birth of that island. I will tell you, for I have come to know that you are one of us.

Wilder and wilder still his death-song rings.

The train stops in the Blackfoot Reserve. A couple of hours delay while the tracks ahead are cleared. Walking around and nodding and smiling. They don't speak English and I don't speak Blackfoot. So this is what they eat – so this is how they live. Pauline Johnson as a Norwegian visiting cousins in Switzerland. The Blackfeet gather as the tourists pour off the train. Pony rides for a dollar – an Indian meal for fifty cents. There is money to be spent and money made. A tourist offers to buy an eagle-feather from the head of the Blackfoot Chief. Pauline Johnson watching a show by Buffalo Bill.

What to do? – what to do? There was nothing else to do. One must always pay one's bills. Put food on the table – pay the rent. All that plodding had worn a deep groove as his path.

"She is kind, she is gentle, she is selfless."

"She sees herself as equal to the whites and Mohawks, to the literary establishment, to the British high caste."

The girl is not of our tribe. She does not know our ways. She married our son against his parents' wishes. They are in love. They are together. She is about to give birth. I have only one tiny moccasin. The other has been lost. I am determined that I will give it to the girl.

Often at the end - questions galore - meddle with your book - know your strengths - the knots are now untied - invited the hostile tribe - the thin thread was broken - the story of her life - would be no unicorns - take it lying down.

Remorse? Yes, there has been some remorse. But you will agree that a lady doesn't talk about affairs of the heart.

Of course, there are poems that come close to giving my secrets away, as you have implied. But they are couched in terms that disguise what is closest to my heart. They could be dramatizations of stories that I have heard in hotel lobbies or, perhaps, from fellow-passengers on the trains.

One is always thinking of relationships. One is always thinking of things about which to write. I take a notepad and a pencil wherever I go.

Kind of you
to think
of me.

A taste of Eva's blistering tongue. Why didn't you fight them? You should have fought them! Why let them take your title away? Mother would have fought them! Father would have fought them! Don't you ever forget who you are! You should never have let them meddle with your book!

Still their rule and council is well meant.

Mother has died. The snows are blocking the trains. I won't be able to make it back in time for the funeral. I won't be able to comfort Eva – she won't be able to comfort me. Mother and Father – the perfect couple. Two as one – one as two. Both were trees – both were vines. Sometimes, when the life goes out of one, the life goes out of the other. Mother has never been the same since Father died.

It was not art – it was entertainment. An evening off from one's personal cares. Every play was turned to her purpose. Every entrance and every exit – moments of heartbreak – moments of joy. Every patron would laugh and cry at her command.

Making progress with the stories of the legends.
I tell each one as if the story has happened to me.

I don't care how hungry you are. You ain't got no right to steal a man's cattle. Don't never take nothin' that ain't your own. I work for what I got. I don't take nothin' from nobody else. I got a bullet that says you ain't takin' nothin' from me. Geez – he's awful skinny. You can see every bloody rib. I gotta think this poor bugger'll be better off dead.

A bag full of gems - perceived from the outside - recognize as autobiographical - every interviewer is eager - dream had now come true - more and more thinking - did anyone notice me - to work him wrong - i might be you - a soul in shadow-land.

One has quite complex relationships with the people of one's life – much more complex than one has with the person sitting next to one on the train. My mother – my father – my first partner, Owen Smily – my second partner, Walter McRaye – my oldest brother, Bev – my sister, Eva – my brother, Allen. All of these people might well have been grist for my poetic mill.

Few of them – you'll agree – appear on the surface of my poems or my stories. In fact, I'm sure it's correct to say that the only people in my life that a reader such as yourself might recognize as autobiographical – would be my mother and my father. They appear as 'George Mansion' and 'Lydia Bestman' in my works.

Why change the names, you might well ask. Well, fiction allows one to make a few changes. Just the details, not the shape – what one ate, or whether it rained on a certain day.

But dip
your hand
in the icy
waters

There was a young girl who had all of the qualities of womanhood. There was an old man who desired her for his wife. There was a young man who also desired her for his wife. The young girl's mother was torn – to whom should she give the girl in marriage? – to the old man or to the young? – to the rich or to the poor? At last, the mother favoured the younger man.

And you listen to their legend.

A country schoolhouse in the winter-time. All the mittens hung on a rope above the stove. The older boys filling the wood-box and a large bubbling, mouth-watering pot of stew. Tempted to cut my act short, so we can all eat. What is race to a little child? I do my Princess – I do my Grande Dame. I sit and watch the children as my partner does his turn. These children have no conception of race. Who will tell them of the fissures that scar the earth?

An arrow speeding through the air.
A stack of poems freshly typed.
A person creating a costume.

Play the roles
of everyone.
What they thinking
when they me.

You had your suit all picked out. Tailored perfectly to your taste. Colour – ease of fit – cut to form. All you needed was a cravat. I was considered and cast aside. Put back in the window, by the clerk, after you'd gone.

Is it true that you are not well?
That your health is not what it was?
That you left the reading-circuit because you fell ill?

Attaching the wampum belts to my waist. People ask me to explain the wampum belt. So, I take a moment in the show and explain what a wampum belt is and what it stands for. I'm always surprised at how attentively everyone listens. They ask me questions – what's this? – what's that? I tell them how I acquired the beads and the porcupine quills. Three or four minutes and then my partner comes out on stage. He makes a joke and then we go on with the show.

Burnt times

suffer through
what now
what do.

People wondered whether she would write like George Eliot.

Dared not walk in day - walk o'er the bed of fire - world lay fettered - the
snow piled up like mountains - sinewy, fierce and fleet - another day set free -
sometimes wonder - my duty lies in self-denial - a dangerous pool awhirl - all
the world to him.

We are edging near the cliff. The people are huddling over our fate. We are the trinkets that people trade. What is the world in which we are living? We would rather die if there is a power greater than love.

A boy with an Indian-relic-hunting craze.
An old man who is starved to the bone.
Rest for chirping voices and tired wings.

A spat with Eva – yes another. Oh why do I go to see her at all? The spitting of venom by two snakes from a single nest. Who can be farther apart than sisters? Two spirited ponies, lashed together – one born for the highest mountain trails and one for the plough. Eva despising my choice of a partner. "A travelling song and dance man! – the lowest of the low!" Eva despising my desertion of the family. "I didn't expect you to come home when Mother died!"

Begins at his birth - boiled beef, strong black tea and bannock - he forgot
all things - the little children grew and thrived - knocked out his teeth - blood
and lineage and nationality - without knowledge of the secret - plunged into
the strange tale - they may be somewhere nearby - hedged about with an in-
violable fortress.

Oh Allen – my brother, Allen. You were only a boy when you left home – as I was just a girl. We met in restaurants and train stations. When I performed, you came to see me, but you never brought your friends. We used to feed the dogs after supper and go for long paddles in our canoes. Calling out across the water as to when we should turn and go home. The water was flowing much faster than either of us could know.
Ahead, the torrent's roar.
Unfinished business. Business that haunts me night after night. I love what I am doing – it is what I was born to do. I have them eating out of my hand. They seem to love me as I love them. I close my hand as I walk on stage – I open it up as I say my first words – it is a gem that I have been carrying around all day. Unfinished business in London, England. I love it here in Canada, but

I can't help thinking that I need a bigger stage.

She never saw herself as a celebrity. Publicity was a chore that she would shun. No one knew what she did when she was not acting. She was never known to give an interview. She said 'when off the stage, I do not exist'.

"She should have quit when she didn't become a major actress."
"Some people become addicted to the stage."

Some things can never be forgiven. There are words that can never be taken back. There are words and there are gestures that show the marrow in the bone. You said that I was not good enough for you. A betrayal of every word you had spoken to that moment. A betrayal of every word you have spoken since. I listened when you said that you loved me. I listened when you said that you didn't love me. I will never – ever – listen to you again.

That's exactly why - communicated all the same - they ask me questions - the silent water of the river - shrinking handful of ice - write the words yourself - never heard any legends - no longer attached at either end - must be heard - dip your pen.

But perhaps this is too superficial. Perhaps you want deeper thoughts than these. The thoughts behind the thoughts, as one might say.

Well, I am not a confessional person. I live my life, as it were, inside. I have thoughts I would never express in an obvious way.

'Private thoughts for public consumption'. I suppose that describes what some people would think is the writer's trade. But a poem is not the same, to me, as an interview.

On your way
up through
the bedrock.

The old man threw a stone – it struck a rock and the rock shattered. The stone had cut an archway through the rock. Every one of the group was amazed at the power of the old man. Then the young man threw a stone – the old man shouted a curse and the young man's stone changed course and struck the young girl's mother and the mother died. Every member of the group was stunned – they were amazed at the power at the old man's command.

Among the merry lads and maids.

Working our way back East. Tiny crowds in tiny towns. My poetry book is old and tired. Slighted in the East, by the literary crowd. Reporters from nowhere checking my credentials. 'When last did you trod the boards in London-town? They say you entertained for the Queen. She's been gone for quite the while. Do you have any plans to embark for London soon?' So – London – thoughts of London – in need of a breath of fresh air to fan the flames.

She danced all of the classical dances. She had a style that was all her own. There were critics who denigrated her. There were others who praised her as well. She was indifferent to any opinions of her art.

When have the rocks of my life not been shattered?
When have I not been standing near a cliff?

"She always liked to play the Grande Dame. Liked to strut across the stage. Felt she was equal to everybody in the world. Enjoyed the luxuries whenever she could. Luxury coach on the CPR. Then a hot bath in what passed, in those days, for a luxury hotel. Then a ride on a buckboard or a mule. Let the money flow through her fingers. Consequently, she was always short of cash. Gave away one wampum belt – sold another. They were historical artifacts – family heirlooms, if you please – but she let them go. Truth is – she couldn't afford to be a writer. Couldn't afford the kind of time to deepen her art. She was always on the go. Stranded on railway-station platforms. Getting late to a town and rushing to put on a show. Tired and exhausted much of the time. Needing a break when things were slow. Had the drive to be a performer. Wrote the poems that she could perform. Didn't write the kind of poems you'd need to read twice. It was all there on the surface of the page."

What we seem to be - peel away the layers - she never saw herself - lived half a life - heavy wings and labouring flight - managing to keep my balance - fifty-one percent of me - if they could know - suffered all the pain - single daring sail.

Every one of us is human. Everyone faces terror at times. Everyone grapples with a personal demon or two.

You say you see me as 'self-composed'. Well – I am – I have learned to cope. I have learned to keep my feelings on a leash.

But everyone – I submit – is human. Fires burn hot in every breast. Some people keep those conflagrations completely concealed.

Pour salt
upon
the table.

Pain is like the loss of a father. Pain is like the loss of a mother. Pain is having a dream burst like a child's balloon. Pain is giving your faith to someone to hold and never seeing them again. Pain is losing your ability to cope. Losing your livelihood and your career. Pain is trying to make one heart-beat serve for two.

Adversity lies at my kinsman's gate.

I am not particularly Indian – I am not particularly white. These are characters that I play on stage. I find a slight exaggeration makes these concepts seem to be real. The audience gasps at my blood-curdling 'ferocious-Indian-voice' and chuckles at my impossibly-imperious 'haughty-duchess-voice'. Sometimes, I think I am breaking-down stereotypes – at other times, I see myself as busily building them up. And sometimes – late at night when I'm exhausted, my feet up on the fender and a hot cup of tea in my hand – I give myself permission to do absolutely no thinking of stereotypes at all.

"I think we'll find her in her work – I think we'll find her in her life."
"The true Pauline is the one that's not written down."

Two lovers

An eagle flying up among the clouds.
A young boy riding a horse through the snow.
A large boat anchored to a rock.

who are divided

Do you feel that you have much yet to live for?
What do you hope to accomplish while you are still on the earth?
Are you intensifying your life in your final years?

by a canyon.

The group was huddled on the cliff-side. The old man stood leering – the young boy and the young girl stood side by side. So what to do? – what to do? – what decision was the best to make? The young man has strength and beauty – what he offers is the purest love. The old man has a mighty power – the rock has been split and the mother has died. As the group huddled, the two young people edged nearer the cliff.

A bubble in the pearly air is seen.

Not making a lot of money – not writing a lot of poetry – not able to finance a visit to London-town. Scrabbling together a dollar or two. Selling the wampum belt that I said I would never sell. So – London again – oh London again – boarding the ship, at last, in Saint John. Now – why would I grasp the hot-poker twice? What embers do I seek to stir again? What flame do I think will be stirred by the breath of whom? Let's hope some things will be different this time – let's hope some things will be the same.

Chapter 9

Pain – what is pain? Pain is that which one can endure. For physical pain I have the doctor – Dr. Nelles, a fine young man. He started life not far from my childhood home. For mental pain – what is the cure? If thinking causes pain, does more and more thinking ease the pain or make things worse? Why does one do so much thinking when one is old?

O! pathless world of seeming.

Arrival in England – again! High hopes for London! – high hopes for London-town! The scene of my triumphs in the past. We stand at Trafalgar Square and look around. My partner is overwhelmed by what he sees. Yes it is the centre of empire, Walter – the city at the centre of the world. Anyone who is a king here – in any profession or any endeavour – is an emperor in every kingdom on the earth. We both jump back as a London cabbie cuts close to the curb.

To be

An old friend who offers some advice.
A river with contributory streams.
A hand which is holding out a gem.

a young boy

Who writes the advertisements that appear in the newspapers?
Do you write the words yourself, or does someone else?
Can every word be taken as the gospel truth?

sitting on a fence-rail.

A little mocassin three and a quarter inches in length.
Starved, crushed, plundered, low.
Firs of giant strength and peerless height.

About love – I can make no observations. About love – I have no wisdom on which to draw. About love – I have no insight which is based on experience. About love – I would have to be guessing if I gave advice. There was a moment at which I realized – and it came as a thunderclap – that I knew nothing about the topic of love – no, nothing at all.

'Til the autumn came and vanished.

Three little dollars. Three little dollars to publish my short story about my mother and my father. But I don't care about the money. It has a vast circulation. It's a popular magazine. Devoted readers are eager to scrutinize every page. I just want the story to be read. I just want the story to be appreciated. I just want my parents' story to be known.

Life went on – he continued to write. Sometimes better – sometimes worse. He earned some praise. He had his clique. Merely adequate is what he thought himself to be.

"She champions her mother's and her father's people."
"She respects her two ancestral streams."

I am walking on a tightrope! I am managing to keep my balance despite the brisk wind! I keep my head up and look forward! I sense that I am at a very great height above the ground!

Nothing but air - a series of links - a betrayal of every word - every stitch is holding - what are the thoughts - doors that will open - can't bear to look behind - i didn't read them at all - seeing all - you are rain.

Regrets? I suppose I have many – but I will tell you about just one. I don't see any point in talking about the rest.

I wrote a short story about my mother and my father. It told, in fifty pages, the complete story of their lives. I called it *My Mother*, because it was she who told it to me.

That story is filled with grandeur. That story is filled with grime. Grandeur and grime tumble like acrobats through life.

*Always know
when you think
of me.*

Walter McRaye comes to see me. Things are starting to boom, Pauline! Orders are pouring in for your books! – and *The Legends of Vancouver* and *The Shagginappi* are still in proof! Pauline-Johnson fever is racing like wildfire! – it's a Canada-wide crusade! The Ryerson Press has picked up on the clamour and is rooting through copies of old magazines! They want permission to print your old stories in a brand new book! Looks like your condition is going to start paying dividends! There will be three new books from you in a couple of months!

O! coward self I hesitate no more.

Taking a flat in a fashionable neighbourhood. A base of operations, if you please. An address that will impress on a calling-card. I want to establish myself in literature and the arts. I have letters from prominent Canadians – people who count for a lot in this town. There are doors that will open to me on their command.

There was another famous actress. She, too, was born for the stage. Her reputation kept growing and growing. Each would read the other's reviews. Their eyes would flash in fury as they read the words.

Making progress with the story of my mother.
It is a story which contains the seeds of my life.

There is a man at the end of the tightrope! He is loosening the knots that secure the rope! I try to move a little faster but the knots are now untied! I turn and move in the other direction but another man is doing exactly the same! The tightrope will not be secure at either end!

Comprehend the forces - quite a story to tell - in need of a breath of fresh air - what has your life been - doesn't want you to have - one last harvest drink-and-dance - every drop of precious blood - shut in a vice - why the man would ask - the groups grotesque.

It's the story of my mother. How she left England and came out here. About the childhood that she was eager to escape.

It's the story of my father. How he served the Mohawk people. How he rose to be a man of accomplishment.

It's the story of how they met. It was the meeting of thousands of years of separate blood. It was the meeting of two young people who fell in love.

And splinter
in shivers
my smallest
of dreams.

Oh I was young and slim at one time. And here I am slim again. All the excess of my middle years is burning away. The cancer is eating me from the inside. A mower moving through a field of sunlit wheat. Taking the flesh and bone of Pauline in swath after swath. The handsomest swells would fill my card and await their turn. One last harvest drink-and-dance before I go.

There's a ghost upon the shore.

These were the golden days of August. They met in Toronto and they were wed. An army major and his wife gave them shelter and love. George's dream had now come true – he was marrying his own true love. Lydia's dream had now come true – she was marrying her own true love. They were perfect for each other. The minister pronounced them man and wife.

A character who is wearing a disguise.
Two people living in one home.
A pool of blood on a doorstep.

Pauline has been
everyone.
Everyone has been
Pauline.

Some would say scars begin inside one – in the heart and in the mind – and gradually, over time, work their way to the surface. Some would say no – they come from outside – they are as thin as theatrical makeup. Forgotten during performance – removable after the show.

Does the advertising distort or magnify some of your qualities?
How much faith should a reader put in your interviews?
Does your public self coincide with 'the real you'?

And now the dress slides over my head. It's actually one of four that I have had since my first visit to London. Barker's department store, on Kensington High Street, is where I purchased most of my clothes. Tea and biscuits while one chooses the latest styles. Every lady was buying dresses – sending the bill to her favourite lord. I almost expected kings and queens to be trying on crowns.

After noon
in life
up joy
down strife.

People wondered whether she would write like Emily Brontë.

Back I flung the bribe - uncovered feet among the coals - I am lost - went out to search - the pathless snow - another day of hunger - wind-blown and wave caressed - my pain will vanish - seethe and boil and bound and splash - bind the broken leg.

I am a man of the cloth. I stand before my God. I do not bow to society's whims. I can see that these two are in love. I believe these two are blest in the eyes of God.

A prince pinning a silver medal on a buckskin chest.
A woman being denied the wines of life.
Crows flying over fields of yellow maize.

Charles Drayton – my fiancé – and I, in a hotel lobby. Crowds ignore us as they pass. We have so much to talk about. Our coming wedding – the music, the flowers, the church. It would seem he expects to talk of something else. I speak first – I hold my heart out in my hand. He speaks second – I am squeezing a shrinking handful of melting ice. After that, there is not a lot to say, so I get up and I leave the lobby. Was he holding out his hand, as a friendly farewell? The street is busy – I make my way. I feel a bump and someone apologizes. I scribble so badly that I have to explain my words. I telegraph Walter McRaye and tell him I've changed my mind about touring. Then I send another telegram to Walter, this time with less of a shaking hand. I ask him to book us out on the circuit for a lengthy tour.

Predetermined through many ages - a quantity of delightful mushrooms - terribly severe and unreasonable - at the stern to guide - beset him from behind - the legends, the traditions, the culture and the etiquette - strong, graceful, comprehensive - we do not welcome them - no one can ever find them - I caught its outline, veiled in the mists.

Eva was very upset when I borrowed money against my share of Chiefswood. She practically screamed that it was our ancestral home. But I needed to have the money – liquid cash – because I needed to go to London. London was the centre of the target for me. I have always felt that my arrow hit the centre – but the arrow went right through. The centre – was hollow – for me. The only question, at that time, was – where did the arrow go?
They had come in peace instead.
No I can't take you everywhere, Walter – some invitations are for me alone. But I shall book us with an agency and we shall be two when we do our act. London is my town, Walter – my town – how many times have I told you that? Simply trust me, Walter, trust me. On my coat-tails – Walter – you shall ride with me to the stars.

There was another famous actress. She, too, was born for the stage. Her reputation kept growing and growing. Each would read the other's reviews. Their eyes would flash in fury as they read the words.

"Some people are only alive in front of an audience."
"Look into your heart and you'll have an audience of one."

I am amazed that I keep my balance! The tightrope is no longer attached at either end! But an interesting thing is happening! The tightrope is floating down to the earth! I am able to keep my balance! The tightrope is floating – gently – down towards the ground!

Tied to time - every drop of my blood - giving your faith to someone - for all the wrong reasons - a double-heart - i simply had to decide - what the stories mean - invites his enemies - some lost melody - help me fend off.

It's the story of their subsequent life. How my father had Chiefswood built. How they spent the next thirty years.

It's the story of light and dark. How we do and don't fit in. How there are forces that seek to undermine what we have.

Eventually everything comes to an end. Children grow up and go out in the world. Death is waiting for every human around the bend.

Dig
to daylight
if you can.

A letter from my mother. I carry it in my purse. Mailed to me – her loving daughter – shortly before she died. I have never looked inside. Shall I leave it – unopened, on the table beside me – when I die? Or shall I open it just a moment before I succumb? What are the thoughts that I should take with me to the grave?

The sail is idle, the sailor too.

Steaming along the lake from Toronto. They were ecstatic to reach their new home. This was the grand estate that George had dreamed and had made. A silver tea-service and a new piano. The hills, the woods, the river. The majestic elms, the sturdy oaks, the regal pines. The brilliant leaves in the flush of late August. The flats on the river, the terraced lawns, the smell of smoke from the clearing of the land. They were sure they had left their yesterdays behind.

How does she do it, people wondered. See the thin ankles – see the frail legs. How can she dance these demanding roles? She is a fairy come down to earth. Surely no human could ever do such marvelous things.

Why did my mother sit me down and tell me this story?
What did she assume it would mean to me?

"She seemed to fit in everywhere she went. Talked with miners – dukes and earls. She could fit in every gathering on earth. Always knew the way to act – the way to dress – the way to talk. No matter who she met, she had a rapport. Talked to people in the London slums – talked to people in Mayfair soirées. Never went anywhere where she didn't seem to fit in. But they always saw her as a visitor – not one of them. Oh she could wear ball gowns and sit in drawing rooms and talk of current affairs. She had made herself quite educated on her own. But they didn't know where to place her. They could only see her as a performer – someone who was imitating their ways. And it wasn't because of the colour of her skin. It was the same among the Indians. She was a lady in eastern clothes who was walking through the Blackfoot Reserve, when the train had come to a stop for a couple of hours. What was she to them? She was Norwegian and they were Swiss. A charming lady – a Mohawk lady from the East – one who was interested in their ways. But in an hour or two, the Mohawk lady was going to climb back up on the train."

Fireworks that burst - the real me - the rock has been split - invisible here on earth - a new note is added - able to keep my balance - those who should know - slow drain blood away - watching a young girl - is this a ploy.

But my regret about that story? The title, as I mentioned, is *My Mother*. But it's about the roots – the origins – the foundations of my life.

Are you ready for the great revelation? It won't seem much to you, perhaps. It's the little things that sting as one grows old.

My regret – my regret – my regret. Well – I would rather be known by *My Mother* than by *The Song My Paddle Sings*. I never managed to put that story on the stage.

Pour salt
upon
the wounds.

Life gives everything it wants you to have. Life takes everything away. What it doesn't want you to have, you will never get. Break your leg – break your heart. Sell your jewellery – sell your soul. You will never get what life doesn't want you to have.

To her 'tis little fortune ever gives.

Oh London – I want to grab you and shake you. A bigger stage – do you hear me? – I need a bigger stage. I have wings I have not unfolded. I have thoughts that I have not written. I am a public person – I give light out and I take light in. I cannot write in a room and put my thoughts away in a drawer. I need a publisher for my poems. I need a stage to read them on. I need a stage – a mountainous stage – on which to soar.

"I don't think we need search for depth in the life of Pauline Johnson."
"All we really need is *The Song My Paddle Sings*."

A raging torrent

Sunlight on the forest floor.
Two performers sorting out their act.
A poem which captures a certain mood.

with no way

Are you aware that many rumours are floating around?
That these rumours concern the days when you visited London?
Is it true that you recited for the Queen?

to get across.

So what do the tempters want? A vaudeville star, Pauline. Touring all the less-travelled places. Topical skits, occasional verses, snappy comments about local dignitaries. And once in a while, you get to recite a serious poem. A tear or a smile for those who live at the end of the trail. We want you to be, Pauline, all the best that it is in you to be.

I have touched your soul in shadow-land.

A son was born to George and Lydia. No grandparents attended the birth. There was resentment on both sides of the racial divide. The boy was the best of both the races. He was the best of both the worlds. A child of the future but not of the past. All the best features of two great races. A double-heart in this beautiful child. His eyes gave hints of Indian forest and English skies.

Chapter 10

A gathering in honour of my old friend, Chief Joe. Sad smiles and happy frowns. A good life lived in a good time with many good people. I say a few words – as many do – but my deepest thoughts are for myself. The tide goes out and the tide comes in. I will write the old Chief's legends as best I can.

Mine is the undertone.

Dominion Day in London. All the Canadians come together to celebrate. A recital at Lord Strathcona's garden party. My partner and I are each called upon to read a poem. Reading again at Steinway Hall and once or twice at social events. No money changes hands – a series of links that make no chain. Plenty of greetings, but no engagements. Pleased to see you – welcome back – we so enjoyed it when you read at our salon in '94.

To be

A person who is suffering great pain.
A poet scribbling on a scrap of paper.
A poem which is buried in a book.

a young girl

What are the factors in deciding what genres to write in?
Does an idea suggest a poem or does the form of a poem suggest an idea?
Does poem or story or legend get closest to 'the essential you'?

paddling a canoe.

A tourist offering to buy an eagle feather.
The young and the beautiful and the good.
Laughing, sighing waiting April.

The old Chief told the story with his hands. The power of the tree – the power of the stone. Every people in the area believes in these powers. They will tell you the story, but none will approach this spot. It is the spot where the witch-woman was thwarted and turned to stone.

He will come again to me.

The London drawing room? Afraid, my dear, you are out of luck. That's a social scene that has faded clean away. People no longer have soirées. This isn't 1894. No more recitals while sipping champagne. They go out to the theatre now – to see and be seen.

Eventually, the greater-composer died. The lesser-composer was approached by a committee. 'You would be the perfect person to speak of our great departed. You are the one who witnessed his greatness close at hand.' So the lesser-composer wrote a funeral oration in praise of the greater man.

"She's every man and every woman."
"She's every child upon the earth."

Lining up outside a cathedral. Didn't expect such a big crowd. Waiting for the doors to open. Hoping to get a front-row seat. They say the bride is an English girl. And rumour has it that she's going to be marrying a red-skin Indian-chief. Hope I get in the front row. Should be quite a story to tell. I bet there'll be war-whoops when the preacher says kiss the bride!

Think more highly - its elevated moments - my deepest thoughts - my needle and my thread - a certain kind of story - what was she to them - the snow is deep - blood on the doorstep - kept in a locket - still he dances.

Over the years, I've had two different partners. Owen Smily and I were a team. We were together for five or six years.

Then my second partner was Walter – Walter McRaye. The two acts were very similar. Only a few times was I completely on my own.

There were two of us on stage. Jokes, skits, occasional verses, then my Indian and Grande Dame act. I had to change costumes between my turns, so I couldn't carry an evening on my own.

I think for hours
about each moment
you think of me.

Eva and the ladies in a raging battle. They are fighting over a corpse. Eva wants to take me home and bury me on the Reserve. The ladies want me buried in Stanley Park. Oh I am too sick to referee this deadly game.

Starved to the bone and old.

Things are slow for me in London. Perhaps if I hadn't been here before. No longer 'The *new* Indian poetess'. No longer 'the *young* Indian poetess'. Perhaps if I were 'the *great* Indian poetess'. But not if I were 'not-an-Indian'.

That is the only advantage I seem to have. There are hundreds, I'm sure, of non-Indian poetesses, and not one of them is welcome anywhere. So – thicker war-paint and a few more feathers. These are the only things that might get me past the door.

A great rivalry sprang up between the two. The presented their plays in the same cities. They played the same great roles. There was a great demand for tickets. Every theatre-seat was filled.

Sitting and writing the stories of the legends.
The sun is shining and there are children playing outside.

I shouldn't have took the horse. We two could have rode on its back. Least then we woulda had an equal chance. Them wolves was howlin' fit to be tied. No way I coulda crossed that river. That ice was all broke up an' the current was way too fast. He shoudna told me to take his horse. I shouldna left him there behind. Them wolves was howlin' an' every drop of my blood was on fire.

Not as swans - no other culture - the one who witnessed - the article has told him - to feel what i can feel - search for depths - highly-discriminating self - labours day by day - singing all night long - just two sparks.

The most successful bit of them all was a skit. It took place inside an asylum for the insane. I performed it with both my partners – it never failed.

So my partner would come on stage. He would say that he'd never visited an insane asylum before. He was surprised that there was no porter at the gate.

And then I would come on stage. I would come on from the other side. And I would say exactly the very same thing.

And I will
float away
on the current
of the icy stream.

There was a witch among the people – she was hatred, war and disease. She moved up and down the coast – she turned every one she met into a stone. She was captured – she was killed – she herself became a stone. If you walk near that stone she will be sure to capture you.

They sing of love and loving.

No, I shall not give up on London – not yet. London is where I have always felt I could expand. Expand my personality – spread my wings a little wider – be more Paulines than I have been able to be heretofore.

A hunter in search of his prey.
A pail of sap boiling over an open fire.
Children who are thought to be naive.

Visit Chief
and visit Queen.
Listen to
the words they sing.

I don't believe that anyone will care to write my biography. I don't see why anyone would bother to try. There is very little about me – the real me – the inner me – that could be known. Eva said, the other day, that she plans to burn my letters. I just rolled my eyes to the ceiling and didn't reply. I imagine myself to be each of my characters. Anyone interested in me would do well to do the same.

Have you thought about writing a play?
Have you thought about writing a novel?
Have you thought about topics that would best be expressed in each form?

Attaching the Huron scalp to my waist – handed down from my great-grandfather. Attaching my father's hunting knife – authentic to him if not to me. Oh, the bear claws – yes they are real, but not authentic. An admirer sent them along to add to the show.

Write down
what tell
tell self
all well.

People wondered whether she would write a major novel.

While I have life - prepare the fire - upon the pathless prairie - underneath them snowdrifts - they scent the trail - smouldering heat of hate - the wild and snarling waves - in vain have sought relief - never a fear my craft will feel - broke the bone right there.

I run my hand over my chest. I feel my heart as it skips a beat. Something, for sure, is happening to me. Is my heart turning to stone? – is my heart sprouting leaves? What is happening to the heart that speaks for me?

The days that are coming and the days that are gone.
A girl who rides through river, bush and trail.
A paddler plunging into the reckless waves.

Yes, Harry, yes – the act that I do can be labelled as 'rather course'. Well – I have learned to toughen up. I have learned to control my audience – I have learned to have them eating out of my hand. Learned to roll them in the aisles – learned to knock them dead – learned to give them what they want. Learned some of the tricks that enable one to survive. Learned to smother the boys in the gallery with a sharpened well-timed jibe – so they don't dare make a peep for the rest of the show. But it's a strategy, Harry – a strategy. Yes it has its 'shallow moments'– but it has its elevated moments too. You want ninety minutes of culture – they find ninety seconds too long. I have to smuggle my poems on stage or there would be no refinement at all. Oh I had higher hopes when I started – I pictured things as you do now. I do not accompany symphony orchestras – I do not appear at The Royal Albert Hall. Harry – you don't know what it is to trod the boards.

His education is two-fold - gleaming horns and shifting hoofs - they would never quarrel again - we both sat in silence - combat against the old foe - the years chased one another - there are no similar formations - too beautiful to mar - sought for many tens of summers - and you will understand.

A man is being beaten. They are clubbing him from behind. A heavy object crashes into his skull. He falls to the ground. He lies on the road in a puddle of his own blood.

It used to haunt me.

A tale of two cities – London One and London Two. The fresh-faced Indian Princess – fresh from the colony – welcome indeed. Here to add a little spice to the London diet for a week or two. Now the aging troubadour – the one who never quite broke through. Making the rounds of the same old offices – some with a different name on the door. Sizing me up as not having a niche – an act that falls between two stools. I just don't see where you would fit in – why not try to hook up with one of those touring Wild-West shows?

A great rivalry sprang up between the two. The presented their plays in the same cities. They played the same great roles. There was a great demand for tickets. Every theatre-seat was filled.

"Too bad someone doesn't turn *My Mother* into a stage-play."
"She could write it as a novel all by herself."

Culture – to me – is more important than love. Romance is the emotion of the moment. Of a life-time, perhaps, but never more. Culture connects oneself to one's ancestral generations. Culture is in one's blood and in one's bones. For her to say that her culture is equal to mine. That all cultures are equal in her eyes. This is a woman that I can no longer love. I acknowledge no other culture but my own.

A jealous snake - I got the idea - that is the only advantage - all with appropriate labels - i hold my heart out - best of both the worlds - she holds her tongue - gathered at harvest time - the chosen me - your tuppence worth.

"Hello", would begin the exchange. "So pleased to meet you. This is a nicer place than I thought that it would be."

"Have you been here very long? Do you know many people here?" We each would tend to say very similar things.

"No, I don't get out very often. I tend to stay inside. The other day I went to meet the Queen."

The only bones
that you will encounter
will be your own.

A young man died in the prime of life. He was generous, warm and kind – he brought warmth and food and fire to everyone. When he died he was deeply mourned. When he died the young man was transformed into a tree. Shade and shelter – sap and firewood – bows and arrows – nests and canoes. If you walk near that tree, he will be sure to give you life.

What saw you in your flight today.

It's the great Buffalo Bill Travelling Circus. All of London is abuzz. After the riding and the roping – after the war-whoops and the blood-curdling yells – after the cowboys have chased the Indians and the Indians have chased them back – then comes the little lady onto the field. Not a cowboy nor an Indian – not a pure-bred anything – and she stands on a wooden box in front of the grandstand and recites – in a very quiet voice – her latest poem.

So – what is a performer? A performer moves from town to town. A performer perfects her art. A performer presents that art to the people of every community. Her art is the distillation of her soul.

What did these stories mean to Chief Joe as he told them to me?
Did he think these stories or feel them in blood and bone?

"She didn't say that she was penniless, but I got the idea that she was. I told her she could stay as long as she wanted to. She spent a lot of her time down on the beach. Didn't seem to want to talk – just to think. It was windy and wet out there, but she bundled up against the cold and stood alone, gazing out to sea. She took a poster out of her suitcase. All of her accomplishments in coloured ink. Said her manager had them plastered all over the province. Said I could have it when she left. It was a very brutal winter. The constant blizzard had her playing to empty halls. She had to pay the rent for all those halls when her trains were delayed. She was thinking of going to New York to see if she could get a few bookings in vaudeville. I shouldn't have blurted it out. I said she was far too good for that – I said that vaudeville was the lowest of the low. After she left, the poster was hanging in her bedroom. The face of it was turned against the wall."

A higher level of thought - an electric moment - i imagine myself - stir memories of thoughts - so little to say - the seeds that he has broadcast - still trying to understand - how leaden was the weight - so bluntly call it - sink so low.

The whole skit was very light. It was just a ten-minute bit. When we came back to a town, people would ask for it in droves.

Two people chatting back and forth. Chatting of weather and other pleasantries, such as visiting the Queen. An insane asylum – a pair of visitors – exchanging pleasantries – all the while wondering why there's no porter at the gate – all the while each thinking that the other one is insane.

People would howl at every exchange. They would be rolling in the aisles. It was all we performers could do to keep a straight face.

Oil and salt
were made
for someone
just like you.

Sometimes the pain goes right through me like a freight-train. The shock is so unexpected and so intense that I am almost numb. I both feel the pain and don't feel it at the same time. My flesh separates from my bones. Every vertebrae pulses in my spine. I go to hell for an electric moment and come back again. By this time, the train is past. I collect my wits and I am normal enough again.

Who has no rest, no joy to call her own.

Feeling down and thinking of Eva. Eva despises my career. Her tongue was as sharp as a butcher-knife, as we stood in her employer's kitchen and we talked. You are wasting your time on the stage! The British see you as a performing savage! – an act that is fit for the London Zoo! – a Neanderthal on hind legs, reciting a poem! Why would you ever choose to go to London again?

"I don't know anyone who can say they've had a better life."
"The great artists are the most miserable people on earth."

A girl

81

Seeds that float and settle down.
A great big bag of emotions.
A parent who is asked his favourite child.

who tells her sister

Are certain art-forms more congenial to an author?
Are certain art-forms more congenial to an era?
Do you feel that you have found your ideal form?

of her plans.

As you live, so surely shall you die. As you live so shall you spend eternity. Shall you be turned into a stone? – hard and dry and without a heart? Shall you be turned into a tree? – offering shade and heat and food for all humankind? Spend your life among the trees. As you live, so shall you spend eternity.
That see so little pleasure, so much woe.
The money is draining from my purse like the sands of an hour-glass. London greets me like an old friend, but what I want is in short supply. What are you doing? – where have you been? – haven't heard of you for a while! Are you still writing those Indian poems? – went over so well in '94! Are you appearing in some of the theatres? – do you have any tickets to spare? It's Pauline – I am Pauline – I write poems and I perform. This is my hat – this is my cane – I can do jokes and skits as well. All of London seems to see me through a fog.

Chapter 11

Why do I think of myself as old? At fifty, one can see oneself as having lived half a life. Check the compass, fold the map, put them back in the pocket and carry on. Go right on through the woods to the other side.

The beauty strength and power of the land.

London – London – London. The water is so low in the well that the bucket comes up empty. What is there more that I can do? Which London rose have I not yet plucked and put in my vase? Is it the duchess or is it the butler who guards the door?

To be a story-teller

An actress who invites her audience on stage.
A marriage which is arranged by the parents.
Two siblings who never have time to talk.

who recites

Do you see yourself as a member of the Mohawk community?
Do you see yourself as a member of the European community?
Would you describe yourself as having no community at all?

the timeless tales.

Traditions which are grotesque in the extreme.
Pale, uncertain candle-flames.
The wash of waves along the strand.

I find life, at times, to be quite painful. I have no idea why this should be so. There is absolutely nothing wrong with my life, at present. Every iron is in the fire. Every finger is in a pie. Every stitch is holding its patch. Every ticket is a winner. My balloon is sailing over every thicket of thorns.

Guiding with her lamp of moonlight.

The short story of my mother and my father. I don't want it to die and be buried and forgotten in the back-numbers of a sentimental magazine. It would make an excellent play for the West End. Johnson Forbes-Robinson – Ellen Terry – Sarah Bernhardt – Eleanora Duse. It deserves to be a sensation in London-town. I would love to see my parents on the stage. Arthur Wing Pinero – Harley Granville-Barker – George Bernard Shaw. So many people who know how to write exciting plays. I should send them each a note and ask them to turn my parents' story into a play.

What is talent? What is genius? What is never-quite-good-enough? His music was played as people chatted. His music was played as they waited for the real music to start.

"She is doing the very best with what she has."
"Top of her womanhood, top of compassion, top of her soul."

I am a little English boy! I am watching a Wild-West Show! The cowboys are chasing the Indians! The Indians are chasing the cowboys! They are living an exciting life! They ride their horses over the western plains!

Make a poem come alive - any tickets to spare - plunging into the reckless waves - the final tempter - what she feels she has learned - a platform for pauline - i should have secured the flap - ballet did not come easy - pathless world of seeming - just a tiny locket.

But – how about you? What has your life been? Have you ever been interviewed?

I would guess that you're in your twenties. Pardon me if I seem to probe. Did you say that this was your first interview? – your very first job?

But of course, life has happened to you. You can't get very far in life without a few bruises – without a few scrapes. Bruises and scrapes that produce the tiniest of scars.

I'm always looking for a new topic for a poem or a story. But of course I don't want to steal your best ideas. You'd be wise to keep your best stories all to yourself.

The little girl
in the audience –
her eyes
opened wide.

They say the books will be coming soon. *Legends of Vancouver, The Shagginappi,* and *The Moccasin Maker.* At the printers and awaiting their run. I am sinking fairly fast. I barely have the strength to care. The plan – so everyone tells me – is to send each copy out with my autograph. This cup of tea shakes in my hand. I don't know whether I will have enough strength to raise my pen.

My heart may break and burn into its core.

Being paid to write articles for *The Daily Express*. My partner idles while I pay for the rent and the food. I told Sir Arthur Pearson that I would be sure to make a big splash. Now I have readers all over London. 'Read all about it! Read all about it! Latest sensation on the London scene! The Mohawk Princess has a word or two to say!' Yes, the surface is a cartoon. Yes, the English is a white-man's cliché of how Indians talk. But I wouldn't be published if I were to write in my own true voice. I write of the white and of the Indian. I write of women and of men. I write of the values of the two cultures. I lock their English eyes on mine. Between us is the armour of what they complacently assume. Then I quietly slip the knife in underneath.

Each felt she had bested in every encounter. Each saw herself as the diva of her time. Her rival was being praised for all the wrong reasons. It was a pity that this was the case. Who could sit in a theatre and not see what was on stage?

Sitting and writing the story of my mother.
The rain runs down the window as I write.

I am a little English boy! I wish – oh how I wish – to grow up! I wish to grow up in a hurry and leave my home! I want to be an Indian on a horse chasing cowboys! I want to be a cowboy on a horse chasing Indians! I want to ride my horse across the western plains!

It is the gem-stone - mode the jewels - tend to say very similar things - all of these memories - all the birds are the same - the magic of the scribbled scraps - present at a special event - starved, crushed, plundered - what story he will tell - all her natural flaws.

You are the writer – don't forget – of your own story. Every story is hoping to turn itself into a legend. Every word is a word that you get to choose yourself.

You can write of you under your own name. You can write with your name in disguise. Change every detail but how much sugar you have in your tea.

Of course, there are things that hard work cannot alter. At a certain level of talent, it will be you no matter what you should choose to write. At another level of talent, nothing you write will be the essence of what I would call 'you'.

Locked
inside
the bole
of this tree.

I have been invisible here on the earth. Not noticed by those around me. Blooming – as it were – in the desert. Exchanging nutrients within a small circumference. Interacting with others long beneath the soil. I was a seed – a stalk – a bloom. I shall go to seed again. I feed the soil – the soil feeds me. Eventually I will be the soil that I feed.

And their voices blend with hers.

The whiskey trade was booming on the Reserve. A quart of whiskey for a cord of firewood. A keg of whiskey in return for a winter's wood. Bible in one hand; bottle in the other. People laughed and called it 'firewater', but the menace grew and grew. The whiskey trade grew to become a dreaded scourge. George was made a government warden. His task was to stop the whiskey trade. Anyone caught buying illegal timber was jailed or fined.

A performance which strikes a lyrical note.
A limit to the topics which will be discussed.
An actress who lets the wrinkles show.

Me recite
my poetry.
Only audience
is me.

I'd like to sharpen you up. I'd like to take you aside and ask you to do a little more thinking. Ask you to ask yourself where you – as an arrow – are heading. Why you – as an arrow – are straying off the track. Why you – as an arrow – are heading off into the weeds. Why you, as an arrow, are lost and gone to me.

What do you think of the concept of 'community'?
Does it mean 'a group of people who share a concern or an idea'?
Does such a concept mean much to you or mean nothing at all?

Shoes and a necklace to top things off. I always keep my English dresses in good repair. I have no lady's maid, as the English ladies do, so if I want them to look fresh, why there's my needle and my thread. I carry an iron with me wherever I am on the road. When one is travelling, one has to learn to make do. One lady saw me sewing on a patch and then descending from the train and couldn't believe that I would wear my mistresses' clothes. I whispered my little secret – that I am the lady and the lady's maid by turns.

Miss friends
people die
feel sad

often cry.

She wrote poems and short stories.

Ankle, wrist and shoulder - unflinching as a rock - a spirit-voice called faintly - been lost fer hours - my sleeping soul - takes his unerring aim - waverocked and passion-tossed - my heart could comfort you - life lacks nothing - all alone I had to live.

We gotta git this injun-agent. Interferin' with the whiskey trade. There's a lotta good money to be made. Trade the whiskey for the firewood – trade the wood for good hard cash. Think we're gonna let this injun spoil the fun?

A flower that hides the scars of forest fires.
The howl of famished wolves.
A little sunshine gleaming through a shadow.

Eva – my personal vulture. She has hunted me down in Vancouver. Shouldering aside my true companions – saying she wants to take me home. "Home to Brantford, Pauline – where we were born – where our ancestors came to stay. I am sure you can be buried on the Reserve." I mumble the word 'Vancouver'. I try to say what it means to me. But I don't have the breath – I cannot find the words. I whisper the name of 'Chief Joe', but can barely speak. I slump back on my pillow and wave a weak hand for her to leave.

You are the real canadian - painted designs of sun and planets - a demon arose in his soul - the sea crept up and up - in determined unison - sighed in absolute happiness - as if dropped from another sphere - a flower that lacks both colour and fragrance - many days and many years searching - the everrestless tides.

A letter from Allen, with a newspaper clipping enclosed inside. His letter repeats, for me, what the clipping says. 'Pauline Johnson, songbird of the red men, will sing no more.' 'And the pity of her illness is that she is in want.' How humiliating for him? – how humiliating for me? Why, my brother, Allen, would you send such an article to me? How did you think that I would feel as I read these words? I have no idea what you are thinking. The occasional visit, on the fly, when I came and performed in your town. We have never sat down and talked over all these years. 'Hope you are well', as a postscript, when the article has told him that I am not.
The howl of hungry wolves.
Three Chiefs on a London sidewalk. A breath of fresh air from home. Here to speak to the great white emperor. Surrounded by London reporters. Flashpowder popping and questions galore. A couple of war-whoops faintly heard

from the back of the crowd. I speak a few words of Nootka. The three Chiefs look at me and smile. None of them speaks Mohawk, but neither do I. I chat, in English, for a while, with the one who is called Chief Joe. A reporter asks me a simple question. You obviously speak the Indian language – will you be interpreting between the three Chiefs and the King?

Each felt she had bested in every encounter. Each saw herself as the diva of her time. Her rival was being praised for all the wrong reasons. It was a pity that this was the case. Who could sit in a theatre and not see what was on stage?

"I wonder which of her poems will live the longest."
"I favour the legends and the stories myself."

I am a little English boy! I am an actor in a Wild-West show! We tour the English provinces! I ride a wild stallion in every performance! I have costumes that I wear! Some days I am a cowboy chasing the Indians! Some days I am an Indian chasing the cowboys! The whole show builds up to a magnificent grande finale! We all stop chasing and take our bows as the music plays!

All we want from you - an idea for a story - not a pure-bred anything - soar to the greatest heights - a pretense of her own - exactly the same reviews - getting a little desperate - o! coward self - tell by the questions - your meaning understand.

Are you married? Or about to be? Took a strange turn along the way?
Don't answer. I'm not really asking. These are not things that I need to know.
So what is your story? No – don't make an answer – I am helping you to decide. It is a question, not of knowing, but of wondering – truly wondering – who you are.

A thousand raindrops
fell
from the sky.

Sincerity at my elbow – in containers. Sincerity in bottles on my shelf. Romance, humour, regret, loss, kindness – all with appropriate labels – all arranged in a row. Powder the sentiments onto the ink before it dries. 'Authenticity' as the bone-and-rag-man said.
Olden scenes that I long to see.
Marshes, miasmas, raging fever. The swamp fever had George in its claws. Lydia nursed her husband as best she could. Then a firm knock at the door. Two elderly people stood on the porch. Lydia spoke only English– George's

mother spoke only Mohawk. George's mother gave Lydia George's baby moccasin. The gulf was bridged at last. Gradually, the fever eased its claws.

A performer gives her heart and soul. A performer is always in danger. A performer is always safe. No one knows what is her heart and what is technique. The performer is always perceived from the outside.

How long did it take my mother to understand her story?
What did this story mean to her when she told it to me?

"I felt I knew her quite well. She was very young when I met her. We met on the canoe-club trips to Muskoka. There were two or three summers there when we both participated. We never met again, but we corresponded after that. I was aware of every stage of her life. Someone said that I was hard on her – well perhaps I was. I've always accepted challenges and always figured that others should too. I told her repeatedly that she should never settle for half. She wanted to be a great poet. She would write to me sometimes when feeling low. I'd say – pay the price – stick with it – don't give in. Then, when her writing started to slip – when she started writing amusing skits and occasional verse on trivial topics – I told her so. I told her that her books weren't as good as they could have been. I told her the performance-circuit was wrong for her. You'll never be a great poet if you're exhausted and travelling all the time. I told her there's always a choice to be made. You have the talent to be a great writer. I told her that in every letter I ever sent."

Is this the path - the pose and the gesture - a very brutal winter - a cage on either side - trust the notes she sends - please consider this - ready to provide an anchor - the seeds of my life - manna falls sometimes - as charming ducklings.

Well, I'll leave you alone for now. Perhaps you're uncomfortable under my gaze. How does it feel to be the recipient of such a probe?

Did I mention to you that I am a journalist too? I've written articles about my people – about my peoples, on both sides. But it is as a writer of poems that I am best known.

It's just that meeting such a young writer. A writer so very young as yourself. Stirs memories of thoughts that have lain dormant for quite a while.

There was
a man
who was blind.

Putting on weight – taking off weight. What is the difference? I am me. The person in the photograph is me. The person in the poem or the story or the article is me. The person who answers the door is me. Yes, and the person who doesn't answer the door is also me.

Brought calm and rest to all.

Two mothers who never spoke. Communicated all the same. Shared the love of the children and the husband-son. What is English? What is Mohawk? They are but languages of the heart. They shared the best of their mutual world. A boy, a girl, another boy, another girl. Mother hens who took good care of the growing brood.

"Well, I don't see why it's so important to be a great writer."
"All that matters is that you know how to write your name."

A mother

Two sisters in the lea of a sunken ship.
A father who is loyal to his tribe.
A performer who hopes to meet the Queen.

who tells her daughter

How would you define the word 'Canadian'?
Have you thought of yourself as 'Canadian' over the years?
What does the word 'Canadian' mean to you?

the story of her life.

Perhaps Chief Joe is the final tempter. Mythical lives of mythical people. Stories of rock and water and trees. Wind in the sails and turbulent water. Trim your sail and turn your face towards the waves.

And shambles home along the country road.

Leaving London again – leaving London for the second time. What did I want? – oh what did I want? I hoped to peel away the layers of the many possible Paulines. Get right down to the bedrock of my soul. Drink deep of the underground currents which are nurturing my roots. Prune away everything but the best and finest me. I sought a cauldron in which to boil my impurities away. And now – again – I am leaving London-town.

Chapter 12

Writing out the legends of the Capilano. Not as Chief Joe has told them to me, but as I think and feel them now, as I sit here, at my window, and write them down. I let the seeds that he has broadcast float gently until they settle down on the ground.

Him who had flung their warriors into graves.

Touring Canada again – touring the length of Canada, for the second time. One more sweep from coast to coast. No city too small – no village too big. No stage too make-shift to be a platform for Pauline. In need of a joke to tickle your funny-bone? – in need of a poem to pierce your heart? Want the agony of the disenchanted? – want the songs of the brave and the strong? I have a great big bag that I drag out onto the stage. All the emotions that I have collected over the years.

To be

A person with a head filled with memories.
A tourist modelling the crown jewels.
A diva washed by wave after wave of applause.

a young girl

Do you write every day?
Do you think about writing every moment?
Are you always working on a story or a poem?

writing poems in a canoe.

A child wandering on the edge of a chasm.
Voices blending in the telling of a legend.
Devouring with savage greed and haste.

The chief was in a story-telling mood. We were walking along, beside the shore. The elders tell of an unknown river – the younger ones search for it in vain. Such stories are told around the campfires. A story is often told of an elk-bone spear.

Bent on bringing down their game.

Serious poetry – performance poetry – costume changes – some topical skits. A few jokes about an alderman or the mayor. I carry them all in my little black bag whenever I make a house-call. What ails you, gentle child? What can I do for you today? Doctor Pauline is at the service of the ill.

Is agony the criterion? He suffered agony, sure enough. He felt he had known as much anguish as the soaring eagle. He felt he had endured as much pain as the greater bird. Surely no artist could suffer as he had over the years.

"She's meeting her cancer on even terms."
"She doesn't give in to the pain or despair."

Awakening all of sudden. Just enough light for me to see. Keeping my quiet and looking around me. A rattlesnake in the tent. Not a foot from the sleeping boy. I should have secured the flap last night. The rattlesnake is deadly. Very few are still found around here. I must move stealthily – or the snake will strike the boy.

Found myself locked - a life-long battle - i am normal enough again - deposited on the dock - refused to discuss the matter - questions cry out to me - a good life lived - thwarted and turned to stone - my smallest of dreams - form circle we two.

Which of my works is my favourite? I don't think of my writings that way. I could never put one poem or story above the rest.

I read of parents who have favourite children. That was never the case in my world. Our parents treated each one of us the same.

And yet each has a different flavour. Each brings something unique to the blend. Each is valued for its contribution to the whole.

The little boy
in the audience –
his grin
from ear to ear.

Walter McRaye comes to see me. So how are you getting along with Eva? Did she tell you why she came here? That it was me who suggested she come? I knew the two of you were at odds – I'd gathered that much over the years. I just figured that in your present situation, you'd be glad to have some help. A chance to reminisce about family. A chance to patch up any rift. You're probably a lot more alike than either of you cares to admit.

My heart is not the only one that grieves.

Sitting alone in a hotel room – somehow it always comes down to this. Passing the night a million miles from who-knows-where. A chorus of crickets outside the open window – a gentle breeze of cool night air. Turning the pages of my book, *Canadian Born*. Reading the poems that I have recited so many times. Recalling the magic of the scribbled scraps of paper – my mixed reaction to the assorted newspaper reviews. So – what do I think of this book now? – what do I think of these poems now? The crickets are trying to tell me something. Is someone reading these poems a million miles away?

My rival is a fad, each thought. She is temporarily 'new'. Great art is that which lasts. She is chasing after sensation. I am crafting a whole career.

These stories are as old as this land and this water.
These stories are as alive as I, myself.

Too much blood. There's been too much blood. The forest floor is soaked in blood. Oozing out of my brother's body. Dripping from my lover's hands. The wampum belt or the knife? What will it be? – what will it be? Will there ever be a day when war shall cease?

The strange thing about dreams - what is friendship for - in short supply - welcome from all the canoeists - the harmony came to an end - the ice was all broke up - denied the wines of life - contained a tiny secret - so complete it seems - so everyone could see.

I wrote a short story and I called it *My Mother*. It is based on my mother and father – on the actual life they lived. Boiled down from the sap in the pail, if you see what I mean.

Two people together – two people apart. A world they share – a world they do not share. The two apart – the two together – then one alone.

So what is this story saying? Fifty pages – a few thousand words. What is it saying to every reader who turns the page?

Locked
inside
this plaster
and lath.

The man had a number of spears in his armory. He hunted on land and fished in the sea. He was equally skillful in hunting and fishing for food. His prized spear was a weapon which had never failed him. It had been carved from an elk-bone long before he was born. It had a woven and plaited and oiled cedar rope.

And she hears her mother saying.

I have never read *Your Mirror Frame* to an audience. I never read it when alone, in my room. And yet I know every word of that poem by heart. It has words that would singe my fingers – words that would burn my eyes. It is buried about the middle of the book. No one ever mentions that poem to me, and I never mention that poem to anyone else. It is as if that poem does not exist.

A writer with an idea for a story.
A knife with a few drops of blood.
A young girl boarding a ship for a new world.

Legends of
a time and place.
Legends of
the human race.

Don't read the reviews – don't read the reviews. Don't brood over what they say. Shallow minds writing shallow barbs in envy and spite. You are only in town a few days. Stay for a month and read the reviews and you'll find exactly the same reviews – about every travelling performer who comes through town. Shallow reviewers leading shallow and bitter lives. A review is a reviewer's review of his own shrivelled life.

Do you write for yourself or write for others?
Does your writing come from your heart or from your head?
What is the best piece of writing that you have done?

Pulling on my buckskin leggings and slipping into my moccasins. Draping my shoulder with my scarlet blanket. It caught the eye of the Duke of Connaught on the day that my late father was made a chief. Adjusting the rabbit pelts that serve as my left sleeve. It was Eva who told me to add the rabbit pelts. The sleeves were a little short for me to wear. The pelts cover what threatened to be my bare arm.

Life gift
what for
give away
get more.

Her poems were published in magazines and books.

Lashed the horse to foam - of exploit and of prowess - his voice is as the dead - flyin' at half-mast - my body and my limbs - and finds the heart - my lone canoe and i - the long long night - the scent of burning leaves - my heart was starving.

I have lost the elk-bone spear. It was a gift from my ancestors. It brought me luck in my endless hunt for food. I will never cease my search for the spear of my ancestors. How could I make a better spear than they have made?

An innocent child who is accused of stealing a cakelet.
Black crows flying over a place of birth.
Watching as wings fade against the sky.

Consider this, Harry – please consider this. Whenever you try a case you are very well-paid. But consider how the public remunerates me. The miner, the logger, the blacksmith, the barber, their wives and their kids. Poor? – destitute? – starving? – certainly not affluent, at all. These people have been hard at work all day. Paid a pittance compared to you. Ground down and looking for solace. I give what I have to offer – an entertaining hour or two. What they want is a little sentiment and some laughs. They pay me with enthusiastic applause. The truth is, the pay for poetry – my dear Harry – is almost nil. Try reading one of your briefs on the public stage. Harry – a lawyer couldn't live on what a poet is paid.

His home-less young heart - her heart is warm for you - you do not acknowledge - the foundations of the world - this opportunity for peacemaking - vitalizing sleep of reviving forces - a colossal base of grey stone - a dream-world of sea and shore and sky - twice, I have seen its shadow - the harbour devoid of water.

Oh Eva – what do you want? You didn't want me to live my life. Now, you don't want me to live my death. You want to take me back to Brantford. I want to die my death here – in Vancouver. You want to be me – Eva – but I don't want to be you.
Night was catchin' up to me.
Life is certainly on-the-go. Now we are being buffeted and cajoled by forces at work inside the mind – now bludgeoned and wooed by forces that come from outside. The greatest city in the empire – the faintest stop on the CPR. A continuous battle on an ever-shifting field.

My rival is a fad, each thought. She is temporarily 'new'. Great art is that which lasts. She is chasing after sensation. I am crafting a whole career.

"She should have stayed home, like Emily Dickinson and the Brontës."
"She'd be a major writer if she'd lived with Eva and their Mom."

He is walking on the edge of a chasm. He is an angel who does not know where he treads. He is in danger from white and Indian alike. The children have no idea of the risk that he is taking. They assume that what we have will go on and on. Play the piano – paddle the canoe – gather for dinner. These people have threatened to maim the horses and the cattle. I tremble every time he leaves the house. I am prepared to never see him alive again.

Me as I am today - slip out through the bars - comparing my losses - other things on my mind - the colour of the shirt - felt I could expand - come in peace instead - acquaintance ever knew - under a layer of snow - were you born here.

That story comes alive each time I read it. I must have read it dozens and dozens and dozens of times. Questions cry out to me each time I turn a page.

Why did they marry? What were their plans? Their expectations?

What their wisdom? – what their naiveté? – what their truth? What kind of maelstrom did they enter? Through what kind of door?

Some turned
to ice or snow

All at once the man saw a great seal. It was of a size much larger than any of which he had heard. He maneuvered his craft to the perfect location to strike. The elk-spear went home and the large seal gasped aloud and plunged into the water and swam for his life. The craft was dragged across the water at extreme speed. A tremendous jerk at the cord and a lunge and the great seal disappeared. The hands were empty that had thrown the elk-bone spear.

The river rolls in its rocky bed.

I always enjoy the lyrical note. *The Lost Lagoon – The Homing Bee – The Lifting of the Mist.* I have a friend who thinks my programs are always rowdy. He seems to think that all my patrons are buffoons. *It is dark in the lost lagoon.* He speaks of them as rough-necks without any tender feelings. *Of hands we have longed for, of arms that entwine.* I've had moments when I wished he was in attendance. *They live along the edge of seas.* A circle of faces in the glow of a dozen candles – leaning forward in order to take in every word. *We two dreaming the dusk away.* I'm sure he would think he'd owe an apology to me.

There is sweat. There is anguish. There are many sleepless nights. A performer rehearses alone in a bare room. Then she presents her works of art to thunderous applause.

Did Chief Joe see these stories as his personal story?
Did it occur to him to write these stories himself?

"Her mother was a full-blooded Englishwoman. Her father was a full-blooded Indian Chief. Her mother wore a gown on special occasions. Her father wore full regalia on ceremonial days. Splendid costumes marked the highlights of their lives. This was the family that she grew up in, but the pageant came to an end. She wasn't English; she wasn't Mohawk. She was neither one of these. Her whole stage-act was some of this and some of that. Elegant drawing rooms – miners' meeting halls – churches and schools – hotel lobbies – everywhere she could perform. She tried – as much as she could – to spend her whole life – every moment – on the stage."

Any self at all - something she needed - he could never soar - cages of greater size - walked through snowdrifts - happening to the heart - the sail is idle - extremely urgent question - all is still at last - cracked his skull.

What is a story? What does it do? And what does it not?

Does it leap right up off the page and seize the reader by the throat? Or does it lie on the lap and purr as it digs in its claws? Or does it serve for lighting the fire – one page at a time?

What is a story and what does it do? – and what does it not? Well, I'll leave all that to others. All I can manage to do, I'm afraid, is to write the words.

*Race
was very important
to him.*

The nice young doctor who gives me morphine. I knew the family when I lived back home. Of course, it was a long time ago when I knew them – long before the young doctor saw the light of day. I hear him coming up the sidewalk. I can see him if I turn my head. I'll just grip the arm-rests of my rocking-chair. I asked Eva to leave the door unlatched. I told her I'd be fine while she went for her afternoon walk. Please, Doctor – I squeeze these arm-rests – the pain is all that I can bear. I am waiting for you to come and ease my pain.

Nor hear a single footstep passing by.

Perhaps the performance I love the most. I am all alone on stage. Come with me in my canoe. We shall go paddling on the Grand. Give me a moment to ship the sail. The wind is lingering in the West. I promise you rapids and eddies and whirlpools. A little danger – a little delight. Don't worry – the current and my paddle will see us through.

"Every member of every group is an individual."
"Your culture is the colour of the shirt you have on today."

A grand-daughter

*A person putting down roots.
Two sisters sharing a modest home.
A person writing a letter of advice*

who doesn't listen

Do you write about yourself or about others?
How much of 'the real you' is in your poems and stories?
Do you dig deep inside yourself or play it safe?

to ancient tales.

The man searched and searched for his ancestors' elk-bone spear. He had other spears, but the elk-bone spear was the best of his hunting tools. He searched at high-tide and at low – would he ever find the elk-bone spear and the woven rope? He had made spears himself, but could never hope to make a spear as sharp and as accurate as that of his ancestors. One night, while camping, he saw a pulsing glow in the sky – was this an omen about the lost and lamented spear?"

The keenest vision can't define.

Gazing out, across the prairie, as the rails click under the wheels – beside the fire, in a hotel room, after the foyer rocked with applause – on the front steps of a schoolhouse where we're staying overnight, thinking of the children playing games. We've been all across this country – over the years – my two partners and I. Made some money – lost some money. Shared some laughter – shared some tears. Packed the hall with a couple of hundred – had a thousand spread out on a hill. Walked through snowdrifts to get to our audience – been escorted from the train. Always a pencil and paper with me – in case I get an idea for a poem. Who wouldn't want to live in exactly this way?

Chapter 13

Let the sun shine through the forest. Let the sun light up the path. Where you have been and where you are going clear in the mind. Meadows, brambles, water and rock. Make a little notch with the hatchet as you walk.

With subtle witchcraft how to work him wrong.

Sometimes rich – sometimes poor. Sometimes a crushing schedule – sometimes not a booking to be had. Sometimes sitting on a bench, looking spell-bound at the Atlantic – sometimes a picnic, on a blanket, and looking out over the Pacific, a glass of wine and a chicken-wing in my hands. Better than sitting in a tiny little room in a tiny little town and wondering why I didn't go out into the big, wide world.

To be

A celebrity giving an interview.
Horses and cabs in the market place.
A person with a mind made of glass.

a mother

What was your relationship with Charles Drayton?
What has your relationship been with George O'Brien?
What is your relationship with your sister, Eva, now?

with a gift of a mocassin.

A wedding ring tossed across a room.
A language for torture and for pain.
Cranes with heavy wings and labouring flight.

Am I dying? Of course I am dying. Who isn't, you might well ask. But am I dying more deeply, more thoughtfully, more intensely than I might otherwise have died? Am I holding life and death – in balance – in each hand? Dying into life and living into death?

Dark its wings and cold and dread.

How many minutes would it take to tell their story? What poems or skits would it replace? What could we do with the fateful beating? What would we cut and what would we keep? I'll talk it over with my partner. I'm sure he'll say that ours is not that kind of act. How in the world can I put *My Mother* on the stage?

He was often asked to speak of the long-dead eagle. He felt he had suffered as much as ever the eagle had done. He had been given much lesser rewards. He had all the pain of the eagle – of this he was certainly sure. What he didn't have was the music or the words.

"She's getting the best out of every human quality she possesses."
"She sees the value in each and every human being."

It is my true and valued friend! He stands in front of me – on my path! He blocks my way and so I stop and look in his eyes! He asks that I should trust him! He says he knows my deepest self! He offers his eyes to me when he feels I have lost my way!

Any more stories - less drops of the me - some foundered and drowned - in search of the perfect outing - bequeath something precious - never quite broke through - to get across - only claim the shadows - sad smiles and happy frowns - don't know his name.

Well this has been a very pleasant session. You have set me thinking on topics that I haven't considered for years. What is a life if the memories remain unexplored?

Is the rain holding off? I hoped we could sit out on the porch. But there's a chill in the air that is not kind to these old bones.

Yes, you may certainly come back again. I have plenty of time to reminisce, now that I make my home here in Vancouver. Though perhaps there's a limit to what you – and your readers – might care to know.

If they
could know
how tired
I am feeling.

Eva sits and rocks beside me. Someone has found her a rocking chair. I have nothing I want to say to her. She says very little to me. Fluff your pillow? Get you a drink? Open the curtain? Read from your books? Every time I open my eyes, Eva is there.

That lion had left his lair.

The one about the boy struggling in snow up to his waist means a lot to me. I don't recite it very often in the program, but I read it quietly, in the candle-light, in my room – often at the end of what I would call 'a difficult day'. It's the kind of poem I would like to have been able to read to my mother. She was a very positive lady, but there were times when such a poem would be a pretty good match for one of her moods.

The tours continued. The fame grew greater. She performed throughout the world. People felt they knew her personally. Every theatre was always filled.

Did my mother see this story as her legend?
Did it occur to her to write this story herself?

He reaches inside my chest! He plunges right on through my skin and into my chest and clutches my heart! He pulls my heart right out of my chest and holds it out for me to see! "Look at this!" he says – "Look at this! This is the heart that pumps the blood that gives you life!"

Face to face - still quite wild - fired some thunderbolts - a precious moment for me - the treasure trove - in a very quiet voice - touched your soul - his death-song rings - come again to me - buy an eagle-feather.

You were hoping for more, perhaps? You hoped I would 'spill the beans'? You hoped you could offer your editor 'a scoop'?
Actually, I think of myself as an open book. All my secrets are in my works. In my stories and in my legends and in my poems.
Some of those characters are definitely me. Some of those characters are definitely not-me. But it would take a detective to figure out which is which.

Seeing all
and doing
nothing.

Sarah Bernhardt behind the curtain. Her arm is trailing out onto the stage. The death of la dame aux camellias. The swan is dying and there is not a dry eye in the house. Just her hand and her arm are making the magic. Telling the story of love – found and lost. The rest of Sarah is chatting off-stage, with her fellow actors. I haven't had a bite all day. What fine meal at what fine restaurant after the show? They barely hear her over wave after wave of applause.
I stood like one shut in a vice.
The children were Indian and English. Learned the legends and lore of both. Two contributory streams. Their mother was English. Their father was Mohawk. The children saw the two as one. A blended future, like the waters of

the Grand. Love of trees, the river, birds. Love of church, flag, Queen. Love of music, china, animals and books.

The question of a title for a book.
A person looking in a mirror.
Two sisters whispering in a kitchen.

Change my clothes
and change my skin.
Don't let
anybody in.

A bag full of gems. A bag full of gems that I wear at my waist. A handful of gems to last a lifetime. If you sell one, lose one, give one away, you will never have another one again. Think before you dip your hand in the bag.

Are other people individuals to you or are they images?
Do they represent the forces in your life?
Are you able to figure out what each one means?

A glance in the mirror to check my hair. My Indian costume takes care of itself. I've had to let my English dresses out a few times. I am no longer the slim Indian Princess that once I was. I am an aging entertainer – a middle-aged public performer – a vaudevillian who sometimes writes an occasional poem. It's been quite a few years since I was the girl who first trod the boards.

Sun set
late day
slow drain
blood away.

She went on the stage and presented her work.

Creek and river, bush and trail - the long trail of fire - never saw her more - the hunter's heaven - me close beside you - the opposite sides of the earth - the love we so desired - breast was born for song - the campfire's blaze - you've come for nothing.

Hope Mom and Dad don't mind. I want to move to the city. More for me there than in Brantford or on the Reserve. Hope they'll always be here at Chiefswood – be glad to come home from time to time. But I see my future as out in the big wide world.

A soul unborn; a song unsung.

A dance on death's awful brink.
A raccoon stealing his portion from the fields.

Eva here, in my home, in Vancouver. Living in my home – not in hers. She has burst in here as if she has a right to live here. To look after me – Pauline – who has managed all my life on my own. Washing the dishes – making the tea. "No – I have no laundry that needs to be done! I have friends, Eva – friends! I don't need you to look after me! No – don't fetch the mail! I can do it myself! I am not so sick that I need to have you to read it to me! You are my sister – not my jailer – stay out of my life!"

The proudest places and heritages - gone to a far country - looked from one to the other - the shadows of centuries gone - never forgiving such injury - its mate is lost - moods of legend-telling - our tribe not like yours - why do you search for it - prowled the length and depth of it.

Mother tried to keep things from us, I know, but we weren't naive. I didn't know that Father's life was in danger, but I knew that his life was difficult. That's exactly why he was my hero – why I admired him as much as I did. We all saw Father's blood on the doorstep that day. It affected all of us – Bev, Eva, Allen and myself – in different ways. When the doctor came, he had to step over the blood. Mother tried, but she couldn't keep us in the dark.

We've raced the rapid, we're far ahead.

The old insane-asylum skit. Why do people laugh so hard? Hilarious laughter at every performance. People ask for it when we come, again, to a town. I worked it up with Owen Smily – then I taught it to Walter McRaye. Two people visiting an insane asylum – each assuming that the other is insane. Howls of laughter followed by thunderous applause. I don't think it could possibly work as a single-act.

The tours continued. The fame grew greater. She performed throughout the world. People marvelled at her artistry. Every theatre was always filled.

"She wore Indian costumes when Mohawks wore modern clothes."
"She wore ball-gowns when women were coming down from the shelf."

"Look at this!" he says! My heart is moving in his hand! He holds it out to me! He stands there with my blood dripping onto the ground! I stand and look at my heart in the hand of my true and valued friend! "This is what I want you to see! This is what has been inside you all along!" I see every drop of blood that is giving me life! "Now put this heart back in your chest and carry on!"

Above the line - knock on every door - to make things just so - essentially self-made - finally put down roots - all of her accomplishments - the edge of a chasm - couched in terms - i think for hours - had all of the qualities.

But look beyond the ink and the paper. Look to the flesh and the blood beneath. Look to the heartbreak and the ecstasy that wells up through the page.

Every one of us lives two lives. What we seem to be and what we feel we are inside. Live by both – everyone has to. Believe in both – well, that can be your Shakespearean flaw.

Better than asking who am I – ask who is you. Have you found yourself in my writings? Where do you find yourself in the Pauline-Johnson world?

Some turned
to water-vapour
and drifted away.

My canoe does not touch the water. My wings do not touch the air. My feet do not touch the pavement or the trail. The butler does not announce my arrival. There is no 'farewell' when I leave. Please bury me six feet deep in an unmarked grave.

Work-worn and old, who labours day by day.

Thirty years and there was sunshine. George and Lydia were so in love. There was love and there was kindness on their estate. Skating on the river in winter. Swimming all summer long. The children would paddle their canoes and play croquet. There was a ceremony in Brantford. George was dressed in his Mohawk garb. The Prince pinned a medal on George's chest.

The broken schedule. The broken heel. The cold dinner. The lonely room. Unknown to those who wildly applaud in splendid halls.

My mother's story has been quite painful for me to write.
Very, very painful for me to write.

"Her greatness was in what she was – not in what she wrote. She was caught between two rocks. Sometimes it must have seemed like a vice. She had no choice but to be simply herself. She had no culture to bear her up. Everyone liked her – and she liked them. But they were all standing on rock – the rock on which they were born. She was the girl who was standing on shifting sand. Every time she moved she was made aware of that. The English liked her – but they saw her as the girl from out-of-town. The Mohawks never saw her as their own. All these people who gave her introductions – all these cabinet ministers and such – all these people who had her recite in their drawing rooms – they didn't see her as one of them. She was a being from another world. And they expected her to go back when the novelty died. So she never touched the earth. She was suspended all her life. All her life there was nothing but air beneath her feet. She held herself up with invisible wings. She was completely on her own as a human being. 'Displaced' is the word that I would use."

Scattered these seeds - look right through my audience - bring the two to-gether - legends that i can trade - is all one needs - the most miserable people on earth - bringing down their game - council is well meant - the words they sing - the group was stunned.

Oh it's so easy to sit in an arm-chair and rattle on, like this, about life. All the wisdom one has gathered at harvest time. An interview as a pleasant diver-sion – a break in one's day.

Unhealed wounds don't seem to show themselves in the elderly. All the fret and haste of life seems far away. All the anguish seems to be put away in a drawer.

But my throat is getting dry. I seem to be doing all the talking. Let's pause for a moment – lest our tea grow cold.

"Are you
the right colour?"
he would ask.

My ship has taken on many cargoes, but the ballast in the hold is rock from home.

We'll wear some rarer jewels.

My face is scarred and my hair is cropped. I have wigs on the table and make-up in a jar. An Indian wig for the Indian Princess – a Mayfair hat for the haughty Grand Dame. I am an actress – I am an actress. I seek to seem what I am not. I die in front of the mirror – I come alive on stage. I am a chimera who only appears in my on-stage dreams.

"I blame the English for not making her feel one of them."
'I blame the Mohawks for exactly the same thing."

Two peoples

A boy sitting on a fence-rail.
A poem as a replacement for a poem.
A girl who leaves her father's land.

who make war

Are you able to comprehend the forces that bring pressure on you?
What are the forces that you have managed to bring under control?
What are the forces that you have been unable to control?

for an unlivable land.

The tempter watches you in the morning. The tempter watches you at night. It sits beside you, in the rocker, while you sleep. Sometimes it is a fairy that hovers over you in the darkness. Sometimes a maggot that burrows into your brain.

If I had thought how leaden was the weight.

Thirty years and there were shadows. The whiskey traders were threatening George. They sent him letters telling him what they were going to do. We'll maim your horses and cows in the fields. We'll burn down your house and set fire to your barn. There's a bullet with your name that's waiting for you. His children never knew. They lived in a bubble of sunshine and cheer. But his wife would always wonder if he would survive.

Chapter 14

Visiting Chief Joe's grave. Soon I will join you in the great beyond. These were your legends – now they are mine – soon others will claim them as theirs. Legends are stories that we tell of who we are. Generations have scattered these seeds across the land.

Wilder and wilder still his death-song rings.

Sensing that things are coming to an end. Feeling old and feeling tired. My day's energy draining away in a few short hours. Unable to get much sleep. Feeling uneasy when about to go on stage. Not the old zip in my performances that I always used to have. Do I want to see a doctor? There is one in every town. Do I really want to know what might be wrong?

To be a man

A person who sits and writes in her room.
A performer who is the toast of London-town.
A person wiping the blood from an arrow.

who gives his horse

Do you feel that you were born to be a poet?
Do you feel that you were born to write short stories and legends?
Do you feel that you were born to write novels or plays?

to save a life.

Winding, half-obliterated buffalo trails.
A man who steals cattle to keep his people alive.
So little pleasure; so much woe.

We stood on the bridge – the old Chief and I. We looked across what I called 'The Lost Lagoon' – to what he had always called 'The Island of Dead Men'. None of our people will live on it now, he said. There was a time when it was claimed by every tribe. The sun was setting on the island as he told his tale.

I like thee well and wish to clasp thee close.

Reciting *Ojistoh* to an audience. Wearing my Indian costume on stage. I am Ojistoh, the wife of the Mohawk. Wife of the man whose arm is iron. Wife of the man whose heart is steel. The man who is hated by the Hurons. Think of yourself as in great danger. Sitting here, on the edge of your chair. Feel the tension in the moment. We are surrounded by Huron braves with no rescue in sight.

Working all night in the light of the candle. Working his fingers to the bone. Striking out as much as he scribbled. Never content with what he wrote. Thinking of deadlines as the sun came up at dawn.

"She wants the best for every person born to the earth."
"She's giving more than she will ever receive in return."

I am riding on a horse. Over river, bush and trail. There are two of us on the horse as we race along. I am the one behind. I am lashed to the one in front. But I am not without control. I am not without resources. I know who I am and what I want. I am waiting for the time when I shall strike.

Her choice of parts - known by the name - sweep them under the rug - studied the works - the everyday person - greets me like an old friend - locked inside - listen to their legend - write down what tell - scrabbling together.

Excuse me – I must have drifted off in my thoughts. What was I thinking? – when I had my eyes closed? Well, you remember, I'm sure, my saying that there has been only one thing in my life that has caused me deep regret.

A number of times I tried to figure out how we could do a few scenes on stage. But it would take so many actors. We only had the two of us, you know.

It just wasn't feasible to do it in our act. I drew diagrams and worked out exits and entrances. I would go to sleep with dialogue running through my head.

How
thread-bare
with the years.

'Pauline' – did you say 'Pauline'? Or was it "Emily'? Or 'Miss Johnson' or 'E. Pauline'? Who do you think I am? – and who did you think I was? Call out to me sometime. Sometime in London – sometime in Toronto – sometime in New York City. Call out to me in Brantford – or in Vancouver – or Timbuktu. Call out to me in the dark on the Caribou Trail. Perhaps I will – or perhaps I won't – call back to you.

And right out into the open stepped unarmed.

It is cancer – yes, it is cancer. I cannot hide it from myself. Well, that certainly explains the aches and searing pains. I'll tell my partner I'd like to break up. Finish the bookings and then fade away. The only problem is that I have nowhere to go. How make a nest when one has never ceased from flight? I fear the increase of the pain. I fear the long slow slide towards death. Well, at least I've had lots of practice being alone.

She grew older – as everyone does. But she never played 'older parts'. She simply applied more layers of makeup. A stronger corset to make her look youthfully slim. 'The most glamorous grandmother in the world.'

These legends are the stories of the Capilano people.
I have written them as stories for the world.

Sittin' here on the porch. Nice to have a bit of sunshine. 'Fraid to sit down less I won't be able to get back up. Here comes that little girl again. Must be comin' home from school. She always comes by at about the same time. Wonder if she'll smile again. She did it yesterday. What would she think if a toothless little old lady smiled right back?

Never ceased from flight - she threw her net - absorbed the wisdom - reading my reviews - a whole new world - what is wrong with you - cover what threatened - the spitting of venom - the only bones - not hiding.

I tried to imagine how it would play on a tiny stage. My partner – a young white male – would play a young Indian male. And I, a slightly older – mature – copper-coloured female, would play a young English girl.

The two young people would be in love. The two would discuss the objections of the families on both sides. Then the two of them would turn and leave the stage.

But where would we go from there? A change of scene – another act. But I just couldn't figure out how to go on from there.

Hearing all
and
speaking
softly.

Warriors hated – warriors fought. Fought with arrows, bows and spears. Pierced ribs and cracked skulls – fighting in groups and man to man. Neither side could gain the victory – neither side could claim the land. Canoes with bodies bobbing in the tide – dead men's blood lapping at the shore. At last, a tribal elder asked to speak.

Seen with mischievous prying eyes.

I have enjoyed it – I have enjoyed it. I have enjoyed almost everything in my life. The highlights and the low-lights – I think they have balanced well-enough. For every day of rain there's been a day which was glorious and grand. There were the gloomies on one side of me and the sunnies on the other hand. I never let either hold me in a cloying embrace.

A writer wondering how to tell a story.
A person who can see what others cannot.
A question that is not quite answered.

Lock the door
and say I'm ill.
Some days
I have had my fill.

Oh I was young and very emotional. The sky was the limit, so I reached for it. Went out on a limb – got my fingers burned – hit the rocks with my canoe. Lost my paddle with the sound of the rapids in my ears. Now I am settled – bland – becalmed. Aware of the hole in my beached canoe. Stanley Park is as far as I venture out into the world.

Do you feel that you were born to be a reciter?
Do you feel that you were born to be an actress?
Do you feel that your life has been well-spent on the stage?

And lastly, never forgotten, but always left to the last – my little golden locket that I have worn for so many years. Worn with my Indian costume – worn with my Mayfair-lady costume – worn with the clothes in which I am Pauline Johnson – myself. Perhaps it's the only thing on stage authentic to me. Yes, the locket with the precious picture inside. Tuck it in where it doesn't show. And with this, my Pauline-costume is now complete.

Weigh self
in scale
balance out
life tale.

She went to England because she hoped to recite for the Queen.

A northern gale - until his heart be dead - hunters lost upon the plains - turns his face - my hot, dark throat - value we failed to appraise - the land of morning - hand almost touching hand - music drowns the day - denied to me alone.

I have asked for peace. I volunteered to ask for peace. Why are the terms so very high? What is gained at such a high price? What advice should I give when I return?

The sports of lacrosse, bowl and beans, and snow snake.
A camper with nothing but starlight between heaven and him.
A single, daring sail in a summer wind.

Harry – Mr. O'Brien. I wish to make a formal request. What was once a baton of encouragement is now a sharpened stick in my side. I have your critique of my recent performance before me now. You could not possibly live my life – and therefore you have no right to judge me. The only person who should sit in judgment of me – is myself. I cannot stop you from buying a ticket whenever I come to perform in your town, but please – I ask you please. Do not send me any more of your well-meant 'advice'.

Claim as his blood-heritage - they will never come again - some of the beautiful customs - the coming of a legend - i'll be ready for them again - at last the gulf was bridged - detached itself from its background - there is something that I want - my ears tingled for the legend - got lost in its very heart.

We used to have bonfires at Chiefswood. Thirty or forty people out on the lawn at a time. Mother's friends and Father's friends. All the friends that we children had, too – friends from the town and from the Reserve. And there would be sleigh-rides in the winter – go for miles and never stop. In the spring, we'd launch the canoes and paddle for miles. Father would fill this great-big cauldron – fill it with water and bring it to the boil. Everybody who was there would pitch in and shuck the corn. Visiting dignitaries – neighbourhood children – take off their jackets and roll up their sleeves. All the faces glowing in the firelight. Some of them chatting and some of them quiet as can be. Thousands of stars in the sky overhead. Nothing nicer in its season than home-grown corn-on-the-cob.

The reckless waves you must plunge into.

Well, what about Vancouver? – the city at the end of the earth. Life on the road is pretty-well over for me. Would this mean a new Pauline? Who would I play? – who would I want to be? – who would I be? Perhaps I could take a little apartment, in a little house, on a quiet street. It would have space for my tea-service and my family artifacts. I could invite people to visit – touring performers and writers and friends. We could sit on the porch and talk about various things. All the things I've never had time for up until now. At any rate, I am finished on the road.

She grew older – as everyone does. She adjusted her choice of parts. She never relied on theatrical makeup. She was acting with her mind and her heart.

She was Phedre, Medea, Electra to the life.

"A writer is a prisoner of his or her era."
"A writer cannot write above the sensibility of the times."

George is gone. No more walks along the river. No more evenings around the piano. The boys are off to the world of business in the big city. Pauline tells me she plans to mount the ladder of literature. Only Eva seems to want to stay with me. We'll have to leave Chiefswood. Can't afford to live in it now. There's a little house in Brantford on a quiet street.

Balanced well-enough - nudged our stars - any question you want - asking for help - to presume on our friendship - sees herself as equal - black crows flying over - it is a gem - the distillation of her soul - her personal showcase.

A skit of how many minutes? A skit of how many scenes? How to present three couples on the stage as the story goes on?

The young couple – Indian and English. The older couple – Indian father and Indian mother. The sisterly couple – English husband and English wife.

How would we manage the change of costumes? The stage would be bare for minutes at a time. And with only two actors – and no chance to use any make-up – how would the audience be able tell when we were Indian and when we were white?

Some of them
caused
the flowers to grow
and some
ruined picnics.

We offer peace, said the leader of the South. You are more numerous – you are more fierce – you are bold and you are brave. We are few – we are tiring – we are running out of food. We have decided to ask for peace. The Northern warriors stood and listened. Victory was in their grasp – why should the Northern warriors ever agree to peace?

His portion steals from plenty's horn.

I've had my dark hours of despair, and I've had my bright moments of illumination. I have paddled my canoe and I've been carried along above the waves by a Trans-Atlantic ocean liner. I've sat in empty hotel rooms and I've sat at sing-songs, with faces glowing as everyone sang around the fire. It was the same sun and moon – the same stars overhead – the same blood in my veins and in my heart. I've been Pauline – for better or worse – every day.

Never talking of her disappointments. Never telling of broken dreams. Not a mention of her lack of a family. Never a personal note at all. Just the date and the price of admission is all she would say.

Nearing the end of the stories of the legends.
It will be a pleasant day to take a walk.

"She was the original self-made person. A scrap of this and a scrap of that. The Indian was more original to her than the Mayfair, because it was the one that was more made-up. Some of that costume was from her family, some was given to her by friends, some of it was ordered from the Hudson's Bay. The Mayfair gowns all came from London – from the season of '94 – but the longer she wore them and wore them – stitching and sewing and letting them out – why the more those ball-gowns came to be part of her. She wrote the poetry for herself. Not the early stuff – that was for someone else – patriotic and sentimental and not all that good. But the stuff she wrote to perform – the stuff that she could recite – that was her. She would stand there in the spotlight – a row of candles or whatever they had – and she would look them all in the eye and read her verse. She was a reciter, that's what she was, not an actress like people say. She was Pauline Johnson looking them in the eye. Oh she had a costume on – but they paid no attention to that. It was Pauline Johnson that they had all come to see. And by god, that is exactly what they got."

To ask for peace - not up to snuff - rooms in buckingham palace - there is uneasiness - every human costume - stores that i have heard - turned to ice and snow - up through the bedrock - oil and salt were made - see the skeleton.

Why didn't I turn it into a novel? Well, my life was so busy in those days, with the one-night shows and the constant travel from town to town. For days and weeks I barely had time to turn around.

I used to be completely exhausted. Some people said that my second book of poetry was nowhere as good as the first. Well, all I can say is that it's hard to write – hard to keep oneself mentally sharp – when one is slowly being worn right down to the ground.

It's too late now. I'm much too old and much too tired to do any more than apply my pen to a few little projects now. It's the one regret – I suppose – that I will take with me into the grave.

No one
who answered
ever said, "No".

I can see my sister, Eva, tending a bonfire. This is after I am safely dead. She barely glances at the pages as she tosses them on the flames. There is a cardboard box on the grass. A silver tea-service – our grandfather's mug. Oh what are you burning, Eva? I can't see the words from here. Did you bury me in Vancouver or on the Reserve?

Today I counted much, yet wished it more.

Ill, exhausted, no partner. A shiver of fear at having come to the end of the string. Looking for one little bread-crumb in the woods. Watching the cows go home to the barn at the end of the day. Where shall I park my weary bones? Where shall I lay my weary head? Where have I felt least-unwelcome in a world that is not my home?

"Write one good poem and you'll be famous for the rest of your life."
"Write one good poem and you'll be immortal for all time to come."

A man

A royal pinning a medal on a chest.
Debris floating in the water.
A person writing a letter with a sharp pen.

who is left to face

Do you feel that you have lived a life of displacement?
That you have been living what one might call 'an alternative life'?
That what you have been is not quite what you might have been?

a pack of wolves.

We have captured your women and children – we have captured your old, enfeebled men. We plan to kill your women and children – we plan to kill your ancient ones. Two hundred warriors are poised and ready at the bow. We are making you an offer – what you must do in return for peace. For every child, for every female, for every old man we deliver to you – one of your best and ablest warriors must die in their stead. We will release two hundred captives on your word. Now – what do you say to our offer of future peace?

We'll watch your fading wings.

Moving to Vancouver – yes, moving to Vancouver at last – moving to Vancouver to stay and stay and stay. All my worldly goods on the train, and very little of that there is, though precious, nonetheless, to me. Farewell, then, to the stage – a farewell, also, to the road. I have loved you – yes, I have loved you. Bare boards in a drafty miners' hall – muddy trails by horse and mule – drawing rooms with brilliant-candled chandeliers. Playing me – playing you – making my costumes come alive. I have loved you – yes, I have loved you. I have loved you simply for this – whether a war-whooping Indian or a haughty Mayfair Grande Dame – that you allowed me to be – while on stage – completely me.

Chapter 15

Break through into the meadow. Leave the pines and the brambles behind. Is this the path that I have been seeking? Is this the way to get back home? How many more miles must I walk until I know?

A story being told beside a fire.

Moving to Vancouver. Moving into my new little home. Careful with the tea-service. It's been in my family for many years. Most of my family things are in that cardboard box. Vancouver is such a lovely city. Were you born here or did you come from somewhere else?

To be an old lady

Acrobats that tumble through life.
A person establishing a base of operations.
Kings and queens in a fashionable salon.

who smiles

How many places would you say that you have visited?
How many places would you say that you just passed through?
What has each of these places meant to you?

at a little girl.

A muskrat looking vainly for a foothold of earth.
A woman putting a dozen men to shame.
Flying upward on borrowed wings.

Leaving Mother's little house, each morning, in Brantford. Walking along the sidewalk to the post office. Any mail for me? – Pauline Johnson? I'm expecting a package from the Hudson's Bay.

A person telling a story to herself.

I don't want the story of my mother and my father to be forgotten. It's buried in the pages of a magazine. A magazine is read and then discarded and read no more. My parents' story is the story that speaks for me. It is a story that contains all that I am. Every rose and every thorn takes life from that root. Their story deserves to be played upon the stage. There are scenes that speak of human darkness. There are scenes that speak of human light.

Vienna was a city of music. A city of music and romance. Not a composer who wasn't feted. Not a composer who couldn't find work. Did anyone know what he thought himself to be?

'She has enhanced her many talents and diminished her limitations."
"She inspires loyalty in everyone she meets."

I have a wish to tell a story! A story that I know I was born to tell! A story that will reach the ears of millions! A story that will summon tears and smiles! A story that will change both hearts and minds!

Not without resources - authentic to herself - the agony of the disenchanted - the crevice widened out - fairies sweat and strain - every entrance and every exit - dark in the lost lagoon - a personal demon or two - so little pleasure - as much as one can.

No, I was never inside Buckingham Palace. Though I had a dream that I was. In this dream, I found myself locked in an ante-room.
A sumptuous room with all kinds of gorgeous fittings. Gold brocade and chandeliers. And the portraits of all these great people were hung on the walls.
The Queen was waiting to hear my recital. I thought I'd better get on the move. So I went over to the gold-leaf handle on the door.

There would be
no unicorns
for the rest of their days.

This brash young fellow sitting here. Does he think that I'm naive? Does he think he'll crack the safe and steal the jewels? I am old but I am wary – I know what to give and what to keep. It's not every woman who falls for a charming smile.
A person judging another person.
Sitting in the tea-room at Barker's department store, in London, and nibbling a biscuit as I sip my tea. Can you believe how splendid this place is? A watering-hole for the ladies and the lords. The latest fashions for the season of '94.

And all this time she kept her secret. She was not what she had claimed. The character on the stage was a fiction. People thought she was playing herself. But the role that she was playing was just a part.

My father's blood in a pool on the road.
I force myself to move the pen across the page.

I have a wish to tell a story! I will write upon the page! I wish to print a millions copies! The sky grows dark and the wind blows fiercely! A storm is coming over the hills! I am attempting to write my story! The wind seems bent on tearing the paper from my hand!

The same sun and moon - passionate, emotional, loud - a rattlesnake in the tent - all had many names - they didn't want agony - put back in the window - hear a single footstep - intensifying your life - had higher hopes - real or assumed.

I had never been in a palace. Though I'd recited in drawing rooms. But this was a far-more sumptuous room than any I'd seen.

But you know the strange thing about dreams. They seem so real to you at the time. But there's something in every dream that seems quite wrong.

I put my hand on the handle. I twisted it this way and that. I couldn't figure out which way the golden handle should go.

Thinking that
someday
I might be you
and you might be me.

Oh Eva, you didn't have to do so much. I could have gotten all the tea-things out. I may not be quite the person I was, but I can still serve cookies and tea. Thank you for giving us our privacy, so we can talk. And thank you for telling me what to say and what not to say. You're probably waiting around the corner to watch him leave.

A traveller moving along a road.

They caught up with George one day. They caught him when he was alone. Six men surrounded George and beat him down. Broken hand, three broken ribs, some broken teeth. Cracked his skull with a heavy weight. Dragged his body into the road and left him to die. George woke up in a pool of his blood. Got himself up and managed to stagger along the road. Lydia came to see what was scratching at the door.

A person who believes that she has no wisdom.
Two blood streams flowing into one.
Old stories buried in magazines.

Open window
soar like a bird.
Mine the voice
that must be heard.

There are scars upon my face. I was deathly ill with erysipelas and it left me this way. I tried makeup to try to hide it, but after a while, I let it go. Felt some shame and felt some pride. How to present myself to the world? Not the face I had as a child. No longer the face of the Indian Princess, nor the glamorous Mayfair Grande Dame. But it is me as I am today – the face that everybody sees – my everyday-Vancouver-Pauline face. I take it with me wherever I go. Don't know what other people see. I don't see the scars when I look out through my eyes.

How long do you plan to stay in Vancouver?
What does the city of Vancouver mean to you?
Did you come here to lose or to find yourself?

My partner and I make a good team. A few jokes – an amusing skit – as a frame for my serious poems. A smidgen of laughter – a couple of tears. Let them out – rein them in. Give the audience something to think about – something to last for a couple of days. I won't be here to coddle them – I'll be off to another town. After that, they'll be completely on their own.

Dark fall
day close
soon dirt
cover all.

She travelled all over the land, meeting people and reciting her poems.

Scarcely see the outline - bends to death - the tempest louder grew - labouring for bread - failed to cool the memory - the wondrous midnight eyes - had we two been discerning - no human throat could sing - the great logs cracking - all tempests die.

It's Eva who wants to stay. The boys don't want to stay home. You take the best of the past. You make the future your own. The only problem is how I'm going to tell Mom.

Boiled beef, strong black tea and bannock.
A heart that breaks and burns into its core.
Sweeping waters, velvet banks, rocky shores.

Belongs to no tribe - half-obliterated buffalo trails - talk not so to me - the rains and mists of late winter - his skull so crushed - a muffled knock at the door - who fought for everything - the secret of her meaning - his longing for the lost island - not much good for anything.

Oh I'm so glad this young man has come. The ladies said that he would be helpful. The only way to sell a book is to 'get some ink', as the promoters say. I have three books coming out soon. This talk will help to give them a boost. Oh I'm so grateful that this boy has come today.

A pen moving across a page.

Eva and I walking to high school in Brantford. Standing and waiting as horses and wagons go by. I have a secret to tell you, Eva. I've written a poem that I want to read in class.

And all this time she kept her secret. Who was she when not on stage? She would always play a character. Did she have any self at all? Had she suffered all the pain of all those parts?

"She wrote in a time when writers swam in shallow water."
"Born twenty years later, she would have been able to plunge deep down."

I have a wish to tell a story! I am standing on a stage! I am waiting for the audience to arrive! The bills are posted! The room is large! The price of each ticket is a smile! I picture a line-up around the block! – up to the hills and around the bend! I rehearse until it is time to open the doors!

The end of the string - what has always been there - a lot more alike - to arrange the itinerary - i thought it looked familiar - check the compass - two snakes from a single nest - the keenest vision - on the edge - thought it was me.

I wandered out onto a balcony. I couldn't believe the size of the crowd. I couldn't resist the urge to give the royal wave.

Suddenly everything went silent. A crowd of thousands and not a peep. I waved some more, but there was never any sound.

I felt something at my shoulder. Someone was standing at my back. I didn't know whether I should dare to turn around.

You are rain
and you are
falling
from the sky.

Perhaps the Chief will come today. Steaming tea in my grandfather's mug. Telling stories by the window as it rains. No he can't – of course he can't. He won't be coming any more. If there are any more stories, I will have to tell them myself.

Two people pouring out their hearts.

George was unable to continue his crusade. He wanted to stop the whiskey trade. But crippling injuries had forced him to slow down. George grew old and he grew ill. Lydia nursed him as best she could. They had caught him at his height and brought him down. The estate flourished, but the life had somehow gone. The children grew up and began to leave home. George went to sleep and didn't wake up again.

Her family life was not known. Not to her nor to anyone else. She knew nothing of the past. Whether peasant or aristocrat. She had made herself into everything she was.

Nearing the end of the story of my mother.
This afternoon, I will take a walk in Stanley Park.

"I think the only time she was happy was when they all lived at Chiefswood. The four children were all close in age. And the parents were so in love. They were the perfect couple – the standard for all her life. She thought the whole world would be as harmonious as her life had been at Chiefswood. Now of course she was just a child. Her mother had braved so much prejudice. Made it seem like the way to behave. But she must have hid the bitterness that she felt. And there were tensions on the Reserve. Her father, who was her hero, had a very turbulent life. He was an Indian, sure as sure, but he stood between the Indian and white. Well that isn't a very comfortable place to stand. Both her mother and father had both feet on the ground. But as a child, she was unaware. Every moment was so ideal. Sleigh-rides in the winter. The ice breaking up in the spring. Canoe rides on the Grand all summer long. Bonfires in the fall with family and friends and a steaming cauldron of corn on the cob. She must have thought it was a life that would go on and on. It was so idyllic that it could never be replaced. What marriage could equal that marriage? What man could equal that man? What woman could equal that woman? What was going to replace that family and that home? I don't think she found a Chiefswood anywhere else."

What you must do - penetrating critical eye - don't read the reviews - becoming somewhat of a skeleton - nothing wrong with my life - show the marrow in the bone - thinking of the children - a london sidewalk - not enough weight - i am a bubble.

It was the Queen – Queen Victoria. With her crown and regal robes. I was taken aback by how short she seemed to be.

I didn't see the Queen as my better. No, I didn't see the Queen as my worse. I looked her in the eye – I had to bend down to meet her, face to face.

I thought it was 'off with her head'. 'This is *my* balcony – these are *my* people'. But she told me to turn around and help her to wave.

And then I woke up. I was in a sitting-room, in an apartment that I had rented, in St. James's Square. I was a visiting Canadian poet – I was hoping to meet the Queen – it took me a while to leave the world that had been the dream.

Everyone wondered
why the man
would ask.

Oh I am in pain. I'm in constant pain. Sometimes I shudder as if I've been hit by a lightning bolt. Of some pain I have been the author. For the cancer I take no blame. But I don't want this young man to know. And I don't want Eva to know. Pain is one of the things I have always kept to myself.

A person trying on costumes in front of a mirror.

Day-dreaming as my grandfather tells a tale. It's a tale for you, Pauline. A tale I never told before. I tale I heard when I was just a boy.

"If there's one person in the world who loves you, then you are okay."
"Providing, of course, that you love them in return."

A man

A city at the centre of the world.
Three dollars arriving in the mail.
Two actresses reading each other's reviews.

who invites his enemies

Is Vancouver the city of the sunset, for you?
Is it the city of the rising of the day?
What does the city of Vancouver mean to you?

to a feast.

One thing about an interview. It's a chance to show your wares. A chance to pump up the box-office. Give a boost to ticket-sales. There's a line in every endeavor. It's a line across your throat. Above the line, you make a dollar. Below the line, you flop. Everyone knows that it pays to advertise.

A boat approaching an unknown shore.

The girl was sitting and talking with her mother. She told her mother that she was going to leave their home. She said that she was going to be a poet. She would take a tour of every major city. She would tour and recite her poems from the stage. Vast audiences would flock to hear what she had to say. She told her mother that she intended to be famous. She would publish her poems in a whole series of books. Who knows, she told her mother, perhaps she would get to go to London and recite for the Queen.

Chapter 16

Sitting at the window when the rain is falling – sitting on the porch when it's sunny and warm.

An old lady watching a young girl.

What better place to live than Vancouver? Edge of the water – edge of the land. Admit thoughts as I care to entertain them – keep them at bay when I'd prefer to be alone. At times, I want the whole day to myself.

To be a performer

A small house on a quiet street.
A palace with a sumptuous ante-room.
A mug full of steaming hot tea.

on the road

If you could speak to the people of your past, what would you say?
If the people of the present understood you, what would they say?
If you could speak to the people of the future, what would you say?

displaying her wares.

A photograph kept in a locket.
A soft and tender voice singing all night long.
An idle sail waiting for the wind to blow.

Sitting with the young reporter at my tea-table.
Three Chiefs on a London sidewalk.
Hard to tell what the story is going to be. Sometimes, when I speak, he writes. Sometimes, when I speak, he doesn't write at all. I have no idea what story he will tell.

The composer gradually grew older. He always managed to pay the bills. The day moved on – the shadows grew. His agonies gave him the dullest music. He passed his whole life in the market – hitched to a cab.

"She gets the best out of herself."
"She invites all to be the best that they can be."

It was just
a tiny locket.

The emotions that I have collected - simply sit by the window - could i
make a better spear - i have something to offer - forgotten in the back-numbers
- to deepen her art - poor tired eyes - what is the water - what was available -
all i needed to know.

Well, thank you for coming today. It's so nice, at my age, to have a chat
with someone so young and so vibrant. Someone starting out on his chosen
path in life.

A young girl
paddles
her canoe.

Walking with Chief Joe along the shoreline.
A Norwegian visiting her cousins in Switzerland.
We are quiet for what seems like hours. We are, each of us, experiencing a
different day. Finally, he turns to me and speaks. There is no end to the stories
he can tell.

I am me, she often told herself. The public has never seen me at all. I turn
Phedre into my character – Electra and Medea as well. They are just parts that
I turn into the character that I play instead of me. The public has never known
the real me at all.

Watching the boy walk down the sidewalk.
Wondering what kind of life he will have.

She used to wear it
on a chain
around her neck.

Endured as much pain - whether the rings still grow - what i have to offer
- i want the whole day - the tiniest of scars - i give myself permission - the bed
of fire - naked born i - to smuggle my poems - freedom to choose.

I hope I have made this interview interesting for you. I could tell by the questions you sent me that you take life quite seriously. May I say that I admire your approach to life?

It cleaves
through the waters
of the Grand.

My grandfather, sitting in his chair, in the parlour.
A beached canoe above a rapids.
My father puts another log on the fire. My grandfather lights his pipe, and sits back and enjoys the savour of the tobacco. He tamps the tobacco down with his blackened forefinger. Is he thinking of a story just for me?

A young poet arriving in London-town.
A group of miners listening to a recital.
A young girl paddling a canoe.

Nail the lid
upon my bones.
My monument
six feet of dirt.

The wheat was waving in the field at harvest time. We went walking and the breeze was cool on our faces. The sun was golden at that time of day. It made the wheat-field glow. We both agreed that we'd spend our lives right there in that field. Then the sun went down and the darkness brought a chill.

Pay the man.
Pay the man.
He makes
a fine pine box.

Is there any way to know what you are thinking?
Do you feel that language is an adequate form of communication?
Do you feel that we have multiple languages in our heads?

Yes, at last, I'm ready. Now I'll just sit and await my cue. While I wait, I'll glance at the mirror. Yes, every effect is in place. This is how I face my public – I have donned my complete disguise. All the me the audience will see will be my eyes.

Grateful me
kind you
form circle

we two.

She got cancer and settled down in Vancouver to die.

Wish to clasp thee close - thro' the forest bounds - a night with nor-land tempest - heat, cold, seed-time and harvest - pearls so pale and cold - what is beyond the border - lay so near at hand - put me in your locket - the night is always mine - i was egypt's queen.

A failure to appraise accurate value.
The man at the opposite side of the earth.
Hoeing one's own little row.

A term for cattle, not men - two thousand acres of land - it leapt into every vein - equal in beauty of conception - blind with blood - succumbed to a raging fever - tumultuous recollections of numerous articles - no more ever come that bad year - did not know the uncertain waters - seem to think it valuable.

I have three books coming out in the next few months – *The Legends of Vancouver, The Shagginappi* and *The Mocassin Maker.*
A man in a pool of his own blood.
Who will buy them? Who will read them? What will my writings seem to mean? Perhaps they'll be read in Australia or Timbuctu.

I am me, she often told herself. The public has never seen me – on the stage or off the stage. I become Phedre when I am acting – Electra and Medea as well. These are the people that I have been instead of me. To the world, there has never been a me at all.

"There's nothing lacking in her work or in her life."
"She needs readers with better eyes than she's had so far."

And it contained
a tiny secret.

Trying to tell me something - some were rescued - no idea of the risk - displaying her wares - my own true voice - edged nearer the cliff - i wiped the blood - the promise of wings - a river rolling along - sever them apart.

Do you agree that the interview is just about over? I can't think of anything more that I wish to say. You know, I feel as if I have pulled out all the stops.

She stops

paddling
and takes
her pen and paper.

Harry O'Brien was a pretty harsh critic.
Family mementoes in a cardboard box.
Nothing was good enough for him. He told me my second book was weaker than the first. Perhaps if I'd written in darker ink he would have been pleased.

She continued to perfect her art-form. She performed on every stage. It was an act of imagination – she was a vision of the mind. She was such a pure performer. It was as if the dancer was not a person at all.

That boy is as young as I am old.
Two stories, sharing an hour and a cup of tea.

A secret
that no acquaintance
ever knew.

That poem does not exist - ghosts walk through each other - neither one of these - i have no idea - the menace grew and grew - paddled their way to the life-boat - costume on costume off - a cardboard box - the candle didn't burn - such a time to choose.

Oh no – it is me who should be grateful rather than you. Perhaps this has been my most probing interview. Be sure to insist that it carry a byline with your name.

She writes about
the song
her paddle sings.

And now this boy is going to sit down and write my story.
A person reciting a poem from a stage.
What is the flesh he is going to graft on these ancient bones? With any luck, it will be a well-told story. If he's a writer, he will make the story his own.

"I wonder what Pauline thinks, sometimes, when she's alone."
"Those times when she weighs the balance – all in all."

A visitor

A girl who is born inside a cage.

A young man interviewing an older woman.
A performer deciding which costume to put on.

who is mistaken

Can anyone else know what Pauline Johnson is actually thinking?
Does Pauline Johnson know what she is thinking, deep down inside?
Is it in your life or in your writings that you will be found?

for an inmate.

Leave Vancouver?
A list of extremely urgent questions.
No, I hardly think so. For most of my life, my feet have had wings. I left behind the joys and cares that brought me here. If I went back for them – resume that burden; drink from that well – they would not be there. We shed the past as we shed old skin. We enter the future as from a chrysalis – we sprout wings that prevent the thought of returning inside. Shall I say that I am Vancouver? – dare I think that Vancouver is me? Nothing as grandiose as that. It's simply that here I am and here I shall – someday – die.

Three Books

Pauline Johnson: Know Who I Am– a novel
Pauline Johnson was born on the Six Nations Reserve in Ontario, Canada. Was she American, British, or Canadian? Was she Mohawk, English, or Mixed? She added up her assets and liabilities and decided that the Pauline the world would see would be 'Pauline the Performance Artist'—'Pauline on Stage'. As for the real Pauline, she would keep that to herself.

The Making of Pauline Johnson: Know Who I Am – a reflective journal
This journal records the author's reflections on the process of the crafting of the novel as it evolved through the stages of planning, writing, editing and polishing. It constitutes an effort to be as conscious as possible of the process whereby the single idea that suggested the topic of the novel was expanded into a complex work of art. Topics range from the nuts and bolts of novel-building to the nature of the novel as an art-form.

Planning Pauline Johnson: Know Who I Am – a planning notebook
During the writing of the novel, the author kept a notebook which records the day-by-day development of the novel as it found its shape and style. The notebook reveals how a vast cluster of thoughts was sifted, selected, structured and polished into novel-form.

The Project
Together, this novel, journal and notebook comprise the twenty-fifth installment in an on-going novel-writing project in which the author is exploring the concept of form and meaning in the novel, and of the novel as a form of expression in the 21st Century. All of the published journals and notebooks are available for free download at www.johnpassfield.ca.

About the Author

John Passfield was born in St. Thomas, Ontario, Canada, and continues to reside in Southern Ontario, near Cayuga, with his family. He is interested in exploring the development of the novel as an art-form, and has written many novels, planning notebooks and journals in his search for a form for the poetic novel of our time.

Novels by John Passfield

Grave Song
The Agony of Robert Chisholm

Jumbo
P. T. Barnum's Greatest Creation

Pinafore Park
The Swan Boat Incident

Water Lane
The Pilgrimage of Christopher Marlowe

Rain of Fire
The Ordeal of Conductor Spettigue

Victoria Day
The Fabric of the Community

The Wright Brothers
Flight is Possible

Leni Riefenstahl
The Valley of the Shadow

Out of the Park
The Cogitations of Babe Ruth

Raskolnikov
Murder with an Axe

Death Day
The Apology of Sergei Eisenstein

Einstein
Wonder

Geoffrey Chaucer
Canterbury Bound

Ospringe
A Visit with Grandad

Pompeii
Vesuvius Dominus

Beethoven
The Ninth Immersion

Job
The Cornerstone of the Universe

Bethune
The Only Person Alive in the World

Terry Fox
Somewhere the Hurting Must Stop

Lord and Lady Macbeth
Full of Scorpions is My Mind

Cyril Passfield
Out West

Glenn Gould
Light and Dark

Emily Brontë
More Myself Than I

L. M. Montgomery
I Gave You Life

Pauline Johnson
Know Who I Am

John Passfield
Saturday Morning

Eleonora Duse
Let Me Have My Wings

See www.johnpassfield.ca for publishing information.

In Search of Form and Meaning: Journals by John Passfield

Each journal is a day-by-day record of the complex process that a writer undergoes while crafting a work of art. It records the largest decisions, of structure and theme, and the smallest decisions, such as the choice of one word over another, and the constant interaction between the two. Each journal is a record of a writer's reflection on the craft of novel-writing.

The Making of Grave Song

The Making of Jumbo

The Making of Pinafore Park

The Making of Water Lane

The Making of Rain of Fire

The Making of Victoria Day

The Making of Flight is Possible

The Making of The Valley of the Shadow

The Making of Out of the Park

The Making of Murder with an Axe

The Making of Death Day

The Making of Wonder

The Making of Canterbury Bound

The Making of Ospringe

The Making of Vesuvius Dominus

The Making of The Ninth Immersion

The Making of The Cornerstone of the Universe

The Making of The Only Person Alive in the World

The Making of Somewhere the Hurting Must Stop

The Making of Full of Scorpions is My Mind

The Making of Out West

The Making of Glenn Gould: Light and Dark

The Making of Emily Brontë: More Myself Than I

The Making of L. M. Montgomery: I Gave You Life

The Making of Pauline Johnson: Know Who I Am

The Making of John Passfield: Saturday Morning

The Making of Eleonora Duse: Let Me Have My Wings

Available for free access at www.johnpassfield.ca.

The Novel as an Art-Form:
Planning Notebooks by John Passfield

Each planning notebook records the planning, writing, editing and polishing of each novel. Each notebook is an attempt to record, understand, and organize the vast cluster of thoughts which occur as one grapples with the various levels of organization which a clear yet complex work of art demands.

Planning Grave Song

Planning Jumbo

Planning Pinafore Park

Planning Water Lane

Planning Rain of Fire

Planning Victoria Day

Planning Flight is Possible

Planning The Valley of the Shadow

Planning Out of the Park

Planning Murder with an Axe

Planning Death Day

Planning Wonder

Planning Canterbury Bound

Planning Ospringe

Planning Vesuvius Dominus

Planning The Ninth Immersion

Planning The Cornerstone of the Universe

Planning The Only Person Alive in the World

Planning Somewhere the Hurting Must Stop

Planning Full of Scorpions is My Mind

Planning Out West

Planning Glenn Gould: Light and Dark

Planning Emily Brontë: More Myself Than I

Planning L. M. Montgomery: I Gave You Life

Planning Pauline Johnson: Know Who I Am

Planning John Passfield: Saturday Morning

Planning Eleonora Duse: Let Me Have My Wings

Available for free access at www.johnpassfield.ca.

Other Books
by John Passfield

Anthems I
Verses from the novels of
John Passfield

Oak Street
The Passfield Family

The Poetic Novel I
Influences and Elements

Intensities I
(1-100)
Verses on Various Topics

Intensities II
(101-200)

Available for free access at www.johnpassfield.ca.

www.ingramcontent.com/pod-product-compliance
Lightning Source LLC
Chambersburg PA
CBHW050150110726
47898CB00008B/2743